Grande Dames of Detection

Two Centuries of Sleuthing Stories by the Gentle Sex

Grande Dames of Detection

Two Centuries of Sleuthing Stories by the Gentle Sex

Selected by
Seon Manley & Gogo Lewis

Lothrop, Lee & Shepard Co. New York

By Seon Manley and Gogo Lewis

Ladies of Horror
Two Centuries of Supernatural Stories by the Gentle Sex

Mistresses of Mystery
Two Centuries of Suspense Stories by the Gentle Sex

Grande Dames of Detection
Two Centuries of Sleuthing Stories by the Gentle Sex

Copyright © 1973 by Seon Manley and Gogo Lewis

All rights reserved. No part of this book may be reproduced or utilized in any form or by any means, electronic or mechanical, including photocopying, recording or by any information storage and retrieval system, without permission in writing from the Publisher. Inquiries should be addressed to Lothrop, Lee and Shepard Company, 105 Madison Ave., New York, N. Y. 10016.
Library of Congress Catalog Card No. 73-4947.
Printed in the United States of America.

1 2 3 4 5 77 76 75 74 73

ISBN 0-688-41551-2   ISBN 0-688-51551-7 (lib. bdg.)

This book is for
Geraldine Pederson-Krag, M.D.,
a true historian of the detective story

Acknowledgments

We are grateful to the authors, agents, publishers, and photographers who have given us permission to reprint the following selections:

The Dublin Mystery by Baroness Orczy. Reprinted by permission of Dodd, Mead & Company, Inc., from *The Old Man in the Corner* by Baroness Orczy. Copyright 1909 by Dodd, Mead & Company, Inc. Copyright renewed 1937 by Baroness Orczy.

The Plymouth Express by Agatha Christie. Reprinted by permission of Dodd, Mead & Company, Inc., from *The Under Dog and Other Stories* by Agatha Christie. Copyright 1923, 1924, 1925 by Agatha Christie. Copyright 1926 by Mystery Magazine Company. Copyright renewed 1951, 1952, 1953, 1954 by Agatha Christie. Permission to reprint also granted by Hughes Massie Ltd.

The Learned Adventure of the Dragon's Head by Dorothy L. Sayers. Reprinted by permission of the author's agent, A. Watkins, Inc., from *Lord Peter: a collection of all the Lord Peter Wimsey stories*, copyright © 1972 by Harper & Row Publishers, Inc.

Family Affair by Margery Allingham. Copyright © 1960 by Davis Publications, Inc.; first published in *Ellery Queen's Mystery Magazine*. Reprinted by permission of the author's agent, Paul R. Reynolds, Inc., 599 Fifth Avenue, New York, N.Y. 10017.

Death on the Air by Ngaio Marsh. Reprinted by permission of Harold Ober Associates Incorporated. Copyright 1939 by Ngaio Marsh.

A Midsummer Night's Crime by Phyllis Bentley. Copyright 1960 by Davis Publications, Inc. Reprinted by permission of Harold Matson Co., Inc.

Finger Prints Can't Lie by Evelyn Johnson and Gretta Palmer. Taken from *Murder* by Evelyn Johnson and Gretta Palmer, copyright © 1928 by Covici, Friede, Inc. Used by permission of Crown Publishers, Inc.

Peter Hampshire for the photograph of Margery Allingham.

Jerry Bauer for the photograph of Ngaio Marsh.

Howard Thompson for the photograph of Agatha Christie.

Our thanks also to Susan Belcher; the staff of the Bellport Memorial Library, Bellport, New York; the staff of the Patchogue Library, Patchogue, New York; the staff of the Greenwich Library, Greenwich, Connecticut; our husbands, Robert R. Manley and William W. Lewis; and our daughters, Sara Lewis, Carol Lewis, and Shivaun Manley.

Contents

Introduction | 11

The Dublin Mystery, by Baroness Orczy | 14

Christabel's Crystal, by Carolyn Wells | 33

The Plymouth Express, by Agatha Christie | 50

The Learned Adventure of the Dragon's Head, by Dorothy L. Sayers | 69

Family Affair, by Margery Allingham | 96

A Memorable Murder, by Celia Thaxter | 111

Death on the Air, by Ngaio Marsh | 141

A Midsummer Night's Crime, by Phyllis Bentley | 177

Finger Prints Can't Lie, by Evelyn Johnson and Gretta Palmer | 213

Biographical Notes | 221

Top to bottom, left: Ngaio Marsh, Agatha Christie, Margery Allingham, Dorothy L. Sayers; right: Celia Thaxter, Baroness Emmuska Orczy, Carolyn Wells.

Introduction

The detective short story has had two great ages, and women have been active participators in both periods. All authorities agree that Edgar Allan Poe was the true father of the detective story. He wrote long before there was a workable police force in the United States (as such police departments were established, detective fiction became more prevalent). The detective story came to real popular appeal when A. Conan Doyle began to publish his Sherlock Holmes stories in the *Strand Magazine* in London.

For a long time women were not active in the field. Then in 1878 an American woman named Anna Katherine Green, who has been called the mother and the grandmother of the detective story, wrote a detective novel called *The Leavenworth Case*. She was unusually familiar with the field of law, particularly criminal law, because her father was a criminal lawyer. Her book, considered "outstanding," was immensely popular.

Although primarily a novelist, she also began to write short stories to fill the ever increasing need for material for the innumerable magazines that demanded her work. In the culture of her era, the reading market was rapidly expanding and periodicals were just becoming the favorite form of entertainment.

The golden age of the detective story was opened by the publication in 1926 of Agatha Christie's *The Murder of Roger*

Ackroyd. Dame Agatha has continued writing novels and short stories throughout her wonderfully productive life, but another woman is equally important. Her name is Dorothy Leigh Sayers, 1893–1957, and we represent her here because she was the greatest historian of crime, mystery, and detection, as well as a superb storyteller.

Her stories present a detective with a well-developed identity, Lord Peter Wimsey. (It always helps if a detective is sharply etched. A. Conan Doyle was careful to give Sherlock Holmes distinguishing individual peculiarities.) Of her creation, Dorothy Sayers said, "If I may refer to him without immodesty, he indulges in the buying of incunabula and has a pretty taste in wines and haberdashery." He is also an example of the eccentric amateur, the detective who conceals his wits behind an aura of superficiality.

Dorothy Sayers, however, was no amateur; many consider her *the* mistress of the genre. She was also eloquent about the artistic status of the detective story:

"As the detective ceases to be impenetrable and infallible and becomes a man touched with the feeling of our infirmities, so the rigid technique of the art necessarily expands a little. In its severest form, the mystery-story is a pure analytical exercise, and, as such, may be a highly finished work of art, within its highly artificial limits. There is one respect, at least, in which the detective-story has an advantage over every other kind of novel. It possesses an Aristotelian perfection of beginning, middle, and end. A definite and single problem is set, worked out, and solved; its conclusion is not arbitrarily conditioned by marriage or death. It has the rounded (though limited) perfection of a triolet. The farther it escapes from pure analysis, the more difficulty it has in achieving artistic unity.

"It does not, and by hypothesis never can, attain the loftiest level of literary achievement. Though it deals with the most desperate effects of rage, jealousy, and revenge, it rarely touches the heights and depths of human passion. It presents us only with the *fait accompli,* and looks upon death and mutilation with a dispassionate eye. It does not show us the inner workings of the murderer's mind—it must not; for the identity of the murderer is hidden until the end of the book. The victim is shown rather as a subject for the dissecting-table than as a husband and father. A too violent emotion flung into the glittering mechanism of the detective-story jars the movement by disturbing its delicate balance. The most successful writers are those who contrive to keep the story running from beginning to end upon the same emotional level, and it is better to err in the direction of too little feeling than too much."

❧ | Baroness Orczy

We are, all of us, armchair detectives. Probably there is no other literary form in which the reader is such an active participant as in the reading of detective fiction. As the (London) *Times Literary Supplement* said some time ago, "It is one of the hectic pleasures of reading about crime that we can switch sides constantly. We can commit murder in the morning and catch ourselves in the afternoon."

Dorothy Sayers said that one of the most attractive aspects of reading detective stories and, for that matter, in the writing of them is that in detective fiction there is a real world of law and order. Justice does triumph; the extraordinary intellect of the detective can discover the *truth*.

We know, of course, that in real life the truth is much more difficult to pin down and that in terms of contemporary police procedures all sorts of modern scientific advances have necessitated the participation of many people in the solving of crimes. But in the creative world of the detective story, the individual detective is still a potent force.

One of the important developments of the detective story was the creation of a character. None has been more important than A. Conan Doyle's Sherlock Holmes. But the "armchair detective" was first invented by a woman, Baroness Orczy. As early as 1900 she created the memorable character of the Old Man in the Corner. He sits interminably in a London teashop, always playing with knots and a piece of string which seems to get hopelessly entangled as he broods about a case, and then the string and the deduction fall nicely into place. Such an armchair detective rarely visits the scene of the crime, but he is always a great thinker who through intuition and deduction is capable of remarkable feats.

Baroness Emmuska Orczy was born in Hungary, the child of musical parents who numbered among their friends Wagner, Liszt, Gounod, and Massenet. She learned English at the age of fifteen, and after studying art in London she began to write only in that language. She married a young student, Montagu W. Barstow, who introduced her to the pleasure of detective story reading and encouraged her to try her hand at writing them. He also collaborated with her on the dramatization of her spy story that was to have worldwide success, *The Scarlet Pimpernel*.

The Dublin Mystery

"I always thought that the history of that forged will was about as interesting as any I had read," said the man in the corner that day. He had been silent for some time, and was meditatively sorting and looking through a packet of small photographs in his pocket book. Polly guessed that some of these would presently be placed before her for inspection—and she had not long to wait.

"That is old Brooks," he said, pointing to one of the photographs. "Millionaire Brooks, as he was called, and these are his two sons, Percival and Murray. It was a curious case, wasn't it? Personally I don't wonder that the police were completely at sea. If a member of that highly estimable force happened to be as clever as the clever author of that forged will, we should have very few undetected crimes in this country."

"That is why I always try to persuade you to give our poor ignorant police the benefit of your great insight and wisdom," said Polly, with a smile.

"I know," he said blandly, "you have been most kind in that way, but I am only an amateur. Crime interests me only when it resembles a clever game of chess, with many intricate moves which all tend to one solution, the checkmating of the antagonist—the detective forces of the country. Now, confess that, in the Dublin mystery, the clever police there were absolutely checkmated."

"Absolutely."

"Just as the public was. There were actually two crimes committed in one city which have completely baffled detection: the murder of Patrick Wethered the lawyer, and the forged will of Millionaire Brooks. There are not many millionaires in Ireland; no wonder old Brooks was a notability in his way, since his business—bacon curing, I believe it was—is said to be worth over £2,000,000 of solid money.

"His younger son, Murray, was a refined, highly educated man, and was, moreover, the apple of his father's eye, as he was the spoilt darling of Dublin society; good-looking, a splendid dancer, and a perfect rider, he was the acknowledged 'catch' of the matrimonial market of Ireland, and many a very aristocratic house was opened hospitably to the favorite son of the millionaire.

"Of course, Percival Brooks, the eldest son, would inherit the bulk of the old man's property and also probably the larger share in the business; he, too, was good-looking, more so than his brother; he, too, rode, danced, and talked well, but it was many years ago that mammas with marriageable daughters had given up all hopes of Percival Brooks as a probable son-in-law. That young man's infatuation for Maisie Fortescue, a lady of undoubted charm but very doubtful antecedents, who had astonished the London and Dublin music halls with her extravagant dances, was too well known and too old-established to encourage any hopes in other quarters.

"Whether Percival Brooks would ever marry Maisie Fortescue was thought to be very doubtful. Old Brooks had the full disposal of all his wealth, and it would have fared ill with Percival if he introduced an undesirable wife into the magnificent Fitzwilliam Place establishment.

"That is how matters stood," continued the man in the corner, "when Dublin society one morning learnt, with deep regret and dismay, that old Brooks had died very suddenly at his residence after only a few hours' illness. At first it was generally understood that he had had an apoplectic stroke; anyway, he had been at business hale and hearty as ever the day before his death, which occurred late on the evening of February 1st.

"It was the morning papers of February 2nd which told the sad news to their readers, and it was those selfsame papers which on that eventful morning contained another even more startling piece of news, that proved the prelude to a series of sensations such as tranquil, placid Dublin had not experienced for many years. This was, that on that very afternoon which saw the death of Dublin's greatest millionaire, Mr. Patrick Wethered, his solicitor, was murdered in Phoenix Park at five o'clock in the afternoon while actually walking to his own house from his visit to his client in Fitzwilliam Place.

"Patrick Wethered was as well known as the proverbial town pump; his mysterious and tragic death filled all Dublin with dismay. The lawyer, who was a man sixty years of age, had been struck on the back of the head by a heavy stick, garrotted, and subsequently robbed, for neither money, watch, or pocket book were found upon his person, whilst the police soon gathered from Patrick Wethered's household that he had left home at two o'clock that afternoon, carrying both watch and pocket book, and undoubtedly money as well.

"An inquest was held, and a verdict of willful murder was found against some person or persons unknown.

"But Dublin had not exhausted its stock of sensations yet. Millionaire Brooks had been buried with due pomp and magnificence, and his will had been proved (his business and personalty being estimated at £2,500,000) by Percival Gordon Brooks, his eldest son and sole executor. The younger son, Murray, who had devoted the best years of his life to being a friend and companion to his father, while Percival ran after ballet dancers and music hall stars—Murray, who had avowedly been the apple of his father's eye in consequence—was left with a miserly pittance of £300 a year, and no share whatever in the gigantic business of Brooks & Sons, bacon curers, of Dublin.

"Something had evidently happened within the precincts of the Brooks's town mansion, which the public and Dublin society tried in vain to fathom. Elderly mammas and blushing *débutantes* were already thinking of the best means whereby next season they might more easily show the cold shoulder to young Murray Brooks, who had so suddenly become a hopeless 'detrimental' in the marriage market, when all these sensations terminated in one gigantic, overwhelming bit of scandal, which for the next three months furnished food for gossip in every drawing-room in Dublin.

"Mr. Murray Brooks, namely, had entered a claim for probate of a will, made by his father in 1891, declaring that the later will, made the very day of his father's death and proved by his brother as sole executor, was null and void, that will being a forgery.

"The facts that transpired in connection with this extraordinary case were sufficiently mysterious to puzzle everybody. As I told you before, all Mr. Brooks's friends never quite grasped the idea that the old man should so completely have cut off his favorite son with the proverbial shilling.

"You see, Percival had always been a thorn in the old man's flesh. Horse racing, gambling, theaters, and music halls were, in the old pork butcher's eyes, so many deadly sins which his son committed every day of his life, and all the Fitzwilliam Place household could testify to the many and bitter quarrels which had arisen between father and son over the latter's gambling or racing debts. Many people asserted that Brooks would sooner have left his money to charitable institutions than seen it squandered upon the brightest stars that adorned the music hall stage.

"The case came up for hearing early in the autumn. In the

meanwhile Percival Brooks had given up his race-course associates, settled down in the Fitzwilliam Place mansion, and conducted his father's business, without a manager, but with all the energy and forethought which he had previously devoted to more unworthy causes.

"Murray had elected not to stay on in the old house; no doubt associations were of too painful and recent a nature; he was boarding with the family of a Mr. Wilson Hibbert, who was the late Patrick Wethered's, the murdered lawyer's, partner. They were quiet, homely people, who lived in a very pokey little house in Kilkenny Street, and poor Murray must, in spite of his grief, have felt very bitterly the change from his luxurious quarters in his father's mansion to his present tiny room and homely meals.

"Percival Brooks, who was now drawing an income of over a hundred thousand a year, was very severely criticized for adhering so strictly to the letter of his father's will, and only paying his brother that paltry £300 a year, which was very literally but the crumbs off his own magnificent dinner table.

"The issue of that contested will case was therefore awaited with eager interest. In the meanwhile the police, who had at first seemed fairly loquacious on the subject of the murder of Mr. Patrick Wethered, suddenly became strangely reticent, and by their very reticence aroused a certain amount of uneasiness in the public mind, until one day the *Irish Times* published the following extraordinary, enigmatic paragraph:

> We hear, on authority which cannot be questioned, that certain extraordinary developments are expected in connection with the brutal murder of our distinguished townsman Mr. Wethered; the police, in fact, are vainly trying to keep it secret that they hold a clew which is as important as it is sensational, and that they only await

the impending issue of a well-known litigation in the probate court to effect an arrest.

"The Dublin public flocked to the court to hear the arguments in the great will case. There were Percival Brooks and Murray his brother, the two litigants, both good-looking and well-dressed, and both striving, by keeping up a running conversation with their lawyers, to appear unconcerned and confident of the issue. With Percival Brooks was Henry Oranmore, the eminent Irish K.C., whilst Walter Hibbert, a rising young barrister, the son of Wilson Hibbert, appeared for Murray.

"The will of which the latter claimed probate was one dated 1891, and had been made by Mr. Brooks during a severe illness which threatened to end his days. This will had been deposited in the hands of Messrs. Wethered and Hibbert, solicitors to the deceased, and by it Mr. Brooks left his personalty equally divided between his two sons, but had left his business entirely to his youngest son, with a charge of £2000 a year upon it, payable to Percival. You see that Murray Brooks therefore had a very deep interest in that second will being found null and void.

"Old Mr. Hibbert had very ably instructed his son, and Walter Hibbert's opening speech was exceedingly clever. He would show, he said, on behalf of his client, that the will dated February 1st, 1908, could never have been made by the late Mr. Brooks, as it was absolutely contrary to his avowed intentions, and that if the late Mr. Brooks did on the day in question make any fresh will at all, it certainly was *not* the one proved by Mr. Percival Brooks, for that was absolutely a forgery from beginning to end. Mr. Walter Hibbert proposed to call several witnesses in support of both these points.

"On the other hand, Mr. Henry Oranmore, K.C., very ably and courteously replied that he too had several witnesses to prove that Mr. Brooks certainly did make a will on the day in question, and that, whatever his intentions may have been in the past, he must have modified them on the day of his death, for the will proved by Mr. Percival Brooks was found after his death under his pillow, duly signed and witnessed and in every way legal.

"Then the battle began in sober earnest. There were a great many witnesses to be called on both sides, their evidence being of more or less importance—chiefly less. But the interest centered round the prosaic figure of John O'Neill, the butler of Fitzwilliam Place, who had been in Mr. Brooks's family for thirty years.

" 'I was clearing away my breakfast things,' said John, 'when I heard the master's voice in the study close by. Oh, my, he was that angry! I could hear the words "disgrace," and "villain," and "liar" and "ballet dancer," and one or two other ugly words as applied to some female lady, which I would not like to repeat. At first I did not take much notice, as I was quite used to hearing my poor dear master having words with Mr. Percival. So I went downstairs carrying my breakfast things; but I had just started cleaning my silver when the study bell goes ringing violently, and I hear Mr. Percival's voice shouting in the hall: "John! quick! Send for Dr. Mulligan at once. Your master is not well! Send one of the men, and you come up and help me to get Mr. Brooks to bed."

" 'I sent one of the grooms for the doctor,' continued John, who seemed still affected at the recollection of his poor master, to whom he had evidently been very much attached, 'and I went up to see Mr. Brooks. I found him lying on the study floor, his head supported in Mr. Percival's arms. "My father has fallen in a faint," said the young master; "help me to get him up to his room before Dr. Mulligan comes."

" 'Mr. Percival looked very white and upset, which was only

natural; and when we had got my poor master to bed, I asked if I should not go and break the news to Mr. Murray, who had gone to business an hour ago. However, before Mr. Percival had time to give me an order the doctor came. I thought I had seen death plainly writ in my master's face, and when I showed the doctor out an hour later, and he told me that he would be back directly, I knew that the end was near.

" 'Mr. Brooks rang for me a minute or two later. He told me to send at once for Mr. Wethered, or else for Mr. Hibbert, if Mr. Wethered could not come. "I haven't many hours to live, John," he says to me—"my heart is broke, the doctor says my heart is broke. A man shouldn't marry and have children, John, for they will sooner or later break his heart." I was so upset I couldn't speak; but I sent round at once for Mr. Wethered, who came himself just about three o'clock that afternoon.

" 'After he had been with my master about an hour I was called in, and Mr. Wethered said to me that Mr. Brooks wished me and one other of us servants to witness that he had signed a paper which was on a table by his bedside. I called Pat Mooney, the head footman, and before us both Mr. Brooks put his name at the bottom of that paper. Then Mr. Wethered gave me the pen and told me to write my name as a witness, and that Pat Mooney was to do the same. After that we were both told that we could go.'

"The old butler went on to explain that he was present in his late master's room on the following day when the undertakers, who had come to lay the dead man out, found a paper underneath his pillow. John O'Neill, who recognized the paper as the one to which he had appended his signature the day before, took it to Mr. Percival, and gave it into his hands.

"In answer to Mr. Walter Hibbert, John asserted positively that he took the paper from the undertaker's hand and went straight with it to Mr. Percival's room.

"'He was alone,' said John; 'I gave him the paper. He just glanced at it, and I thought he looked rather astonished, but he said nothing, and I at once left the room.'

"'When you say that you recognized the paper as the one which you had seen your master sign the day before, how did you actually recognize that it was the same paper?' asked Mr. Hibbert amidst breathless interest on the part of the spectators.

"'It looked exactly the same paper to me, sir,' replied John, somewhat vaguely.

"'Did you look at the contents, then?'

"'No, sir; certainly not.'

"'Had you done so the day before?'

"'No, sir, only at my master's signature.'

"'Then you only thought by the *outside* look of the paper that it was the same?'

"'It looked the same thing, sir,' persisted John obstinately.

"You see," continued the man in the corner, leaning eagerly forward across the narrow marble table, "the contention of Murray Brooks's adviser was that Mr. Brooks, having made a will and hidden it—for some reason or other under his pillow—that will had fallen, through the means related by John O'Neill, into the hands of Mr. Percival Brooks, who had destroyed it and substituted a forged one in its place, which adjudged the whole of Mr. Brooks's millions to himself. It was a terrible and daring accusation directed against a gentleman who, in spite of his many wild oats sowed in early youth, was a prominent and important figure in Irish high life.

"But John O'Neill had not finished his evidence, and Mr. Walter Hibbert had a bit of sensation still up his sleeve. He had, namely, produced a paper, the will proved by Mr. Percival Brooks, and had asked John O'Neill if once again he recognized the paper.

"'Certainly, sir,' said John unhesitatingly, 'this is the one the undertaker found under my poor dead master's pillow, and which I took to Mr. Percival's room immediately.'

"Then the paper was unfolded and placed before the witness.

" 'Now, Mr. O'Neill, will you tell me if that is your signature?'

"John looked at it for a moment; then he said: 'Excuse me, sir,' and produced a pair of spectacles which he carefully adjusted before he again examined the paper. Then he thoughtfully shook his head.

" 'It don't look much like my writing, sir,' he said at last. 'That is to say,' he added, by way of elucidating the matter, 'it does look like my writing, but then I don't think it is.'

"The learned counsel," continued the old man in the corner, "went on arguing, speechifying, cross-examining for nearly a week, until they arrived at the one conclusion which was inevitable from the very first, namely, that the will *was* a forgery—a gross, clumsy, idiotic forgery, since both John O'Neill and Pat Mooney, the two witnesses, absolutely repudiated the signatures as their own. The only successful bit of calligraphy the forger had done was the signature of old Mr. Brooks.

"It was a very curious fact, and one which had undoubtedly aided the forger in accomplishing his work quickly, that Mr. Wethered the lawyer, having, no doubt, realized that Mr. Brooks had not many moments in life to spare, had not drawn up the usual engrossed, magnificent document dear to the lawyer heart, but had used for his client's will one of those regular printed forms which can be purchased at any stationer's.

"Mr. Percival Brooks, of course, flatly denied the serious allegation brought against him. He admitted that the butler had brought him the document the morning after his father's death, and that he certainly, on glancing at it, had been very much astonished to see that that document was his father's will. Against that he declared that its contents did not astonish him in the slightest degree, that he himself knew of the testator's intentions, but that he certainly thought his father had entrusted the will to the care of Mr. Wethered, who did all his business for him.

" 'I only very cursorily glanced at the signature,' he concluded, speaking in a perfectly calm, clear voice; 'you must understand that the thought of forgery was very far from my mind, and that my father's signature is exceedingly well imitated, if, indeed, it is not his own, which I am not at all prepared to believe. As for the two witnesses' signatures, I don't think I had ever seen them before. I took the document to Messrs. Barkston and Maud, who had often done business for me before, and they assured me that the will was in perfect form and order.'

"Asked why he had not entrusted the will to his father's solicitors, he replied:

" 'For the very simple reason that exactly half an hour before the will was placed in my hands, I had read that Mr. Patrick Wethered had been murdered the night before. Mr. Hibbert, the junior partner, was not personally known to me.'

"After that, for form's sake, a good deal of expert evidence was heard on the subject of the dead man's signature. But that was quite unanimous, and merely went to corroborate what had already been established beyond a doubt, namely, that the will dated February 1st, 1908, was a forgery, and probate of the will dated 1891 was therefore granted to Mr. Murray Brooks, the sole executor mentioned therein.

"Two days later the police applied for a warrant for the arrest of Mr. Percival Brooks on a charge of forgery.

"The Crown prosecuted, and Mr. Brooks had again the support of Mr. Oranmore, the eminent K.C. Perfectly calm, like a man conscious of his own innocence and unable to grasp the idea that justice does sometimes miscarry, Mr. Brooks, the son of the millionaire, himself still the possessor of a very large fortune under the former will, stood up in the dock on that memorable day in October, 1908, which still no doubt lives in the memory of his many friends.

"All the evidence with regard to Mr. Brooks's last moments and the forged will was gone through over again. That will, it was the contention of the Crown, had been forged so entirely in favor of the accused, cutting out everyone else, that obviously no one but the beneficiary under that false will would have had any motive in forging it.

"Very pale, and with a frown between his deep-set, handsome Irish eyes, Percival Brooks listened to this large volume of evidence piled up against him by the Crown.

"At times he held brief consultations with Mr. Oranmore, who seemed as cool as a cucumber. Have you ever seen Oranmore in court? He is a character worthy of Dickens. His pronounced brogue, his fat, podgy, clean-shaven face, his not always immaculately clean large hands, have often delighted the caricaturist. As it very soon transpired during that memorable magisterial inquiry, he relied for a verdict in favor of his client upon two main points, and he had concentrated all his skill upon making these two points as telling as he possibly could.

"The first point was the question of time. John O'Neill, cross-examined by Oranmore, stated without hesitation that he had given the will to Mr. Percival at eleven o'clock in the morning. And now the eminent K.C. brought forward and placed in the witness box the very lawyers into whose hands the accused had then immediately placed the will. Now, Mr. Barkston, a very well-known solicitor of King Street, declared positively that Mr. Percival Brooks was in his office at a quarter before twelve; two of his clerks testified to the same time exactly, and it was *impossible*, contended Mr. Oranmore, that within three-quarters of an hour Mr. Brooks could have gone to a stationer's, bought a will form, copied Mr. Wethered's writing, his father's signature, and that of John O'Neill and Pat Mooney.

"Such a thing might have been planned, arranged, practiced, and ultimately, after a great deal of trouble, successfully carried out, but human intelligence could not grasp the other as a possibility.

"Still the judge wavered. The eminent K.C. had shaken but not shattered his belief in the prisoner's guilt. But there was one point more, and this Oranmore, with the skill of a dramatist, had reserved for the fall of the curtain.

"He noted every sign in the judge's face, he guessed that his client was not yet absolutely safe, then only did he produce his last two witnesses.

"One of them was Mary Sullivan, one of the housemaids in the Fitzwilliam mansion. She had been sent up by the cook at a quarter past four o'clock on the afternoon of February 1st with some hot water, which the nurse had ordered, for the master's room. Just as she was about to knock at the door Mr. Wethered was coming out of the room. Mary stopped with the tray in her hand, and at the door Mr. Wethered turned and said quite loudly: 'Now, don't fret, don't be anxious; do try and be calm. Your will is safe in my pocket, nothing can change it or alter one word of it but yourself.'

"It was, of course, a very ticklish point in law whether the housemaid's evidence could be accepted. You see, she was quoting the words of a man since dead, spoken to another man also dead. There is no doubt that had there been very strong evidence on the other side against Percival Brooks, Mary Sullivan's would have counted for nothing; but, as I told you before, the judge's belief in the prisoner's guilt was already very seriously shaken, and now the final blow aimed at it by Mr. Oranmore shattered his last lingering doubts.

"Dr. Mulligan, namely, had been placed by Mr. Oranmore into the witness box. He was a medical man of unimpeachable authority, in fact, absolutely at the head of his profession in Dublin. What he said practically corroborated Mary Sullivan's testimony. He had gone in to see Mr. Brooks at half-past four, and understood from him that his lawyer had just left him.

"Mr. Brooks certainly, though terribly weak, was calm and more composed. He was dying from a sudden heart attack, and Dr. Mulligan foresaw the almost immediate end. But he was still conscious and managed to murmur feebly: 'I feel much easier in my mind now, doctor—I have made my will—Wethered has been—he's got it in his pocket—it is safe there—safe from that—' But the words died on his lips, and after that he spoke but little. He saw his two sons before he died, but hardly knew them or even looked at them.

"You see," concluded the man in the corner, "you see that the prosecution was bound to collapse. Oranmore did not give it a leg to stand on. The will was forged, it is true, forged in the favor of Percival Brooks and of no one else, forged for him and for his benefit. Whether he knew and connived at the forgery was never proved or, as far as I know, even hinted, but it was impossible to go against all the evidence, which pointed that, as far as the act itself was concerned, he at least was innocent. You see, Dr. Mulligan's evidence was not to be shaken. Mary Sullivan's was equally strong.

"There were two witnesses swearing positively that old Brooks's will was in Mr. Wethered's keeping when that gentleman left the Fitzwilliam mansion at a quarter past four. At five o'clock in the afternoon the lawyer was found dead in Phoenix Park. Between a quarter past four and eight o'clock in the evening Percival Brooks never left the house—that was subsequently proved by Oranmore up to the hilt and beyond a doubt. Since the will found under old Brooks's pillow was a forged will, where then was the will he did make, and which Wethered carried away with him in his pocket?"

"Stolen, of course," said Polly, "by those who murdered and robbed him; it may have been of no value to them, but they naturally would destroy it, lest it might prove a clew against them."

"Then you think it was mere coincidence?" he asked excitedly.

"What?"

"That Wethered was murdered and robbed at the very moment that he carried the will in his pocket, whilst another was being forged in its place?"

"It certainly would be very curious, if it *were* a coincidence," she said musingly.

"Very," he repeated with biting sarcasm, whilst nervously his bony fingers played with the inevitable bit of string. "Very curious indeed. Just think of the whole thing. There was the old man with all his wealth, and two sons, one to whom he is devoted, and the other with whom he does nothing but quarrel. One day there is another of these quarrels, but more violent, more terrible than any that have previously occurred, with the result that the father, heartbroken by it all, has an attack of apoplexy and practically dies of a broken heart. After that he alters his will, and subsequently a will is proved which turns out to be a forgery.

"Now everybody—police, press, and public alike—at once jump to the conclusion that, as Percival Brooks benefits by that forged will, Percival Brooks must be the forger."

"Seek for him whom the crime benefits, is your own axiom," argued the girl.

"I beg your pardon?"

"Percival Brooks benefited to the tune of £2,000,000."

"I beg your pardon. He did nothing of the sort. He was left

with less than half the share that his younger brother inherited."

"Now, yes; but that was a former will and—"

"And that forged will was so clumsily executed, the signature so carelessly imitated, that the forgery was bound to come to light. Did *that* never strike you?"

"Yes, but—"

"There is no but," he interrupted. "It was all as clear as daylight to me from the very first. The quarrel with the old man, which broke his heart, was not with his eldest son, with whom he was used to quarreling, but with the second son whom he idolized, in whom he believed. Don't you remember how John O'Neill heard the words 'liar' and 'deceit'? Percival Brooks had never deceived his father. His sins were all on the surface. Murray had led a quiet life, had pandered to his father, and fawned upon him, until, like most hypocrites, he at last got found out. Who knows what ugly gambling debt or debt of honor, suddenly revealed to old Brooks, was the cause of that last and deadly quarrel?

"You remember that it was Percival who remained beside his father and carried him up to his room. Where was Murray throughout that long and painful day, when his father lay dying—he, the idolized son, the apple of the old man's eye? You never hear his name mentioned as being present there all that day. But he knew that he had offended his father mortally, and that his father meant to cut him off with a shilling. He knew that Mr. Wethered had been sent for, that Wethered left the house soon after four o'clock.

"And here the cleverness of the man comes in. Having lain in wait for Wethered and knocked him on the back of the head with a stick, he could not very well make that will disappear altogether. There remained the faint chance of some other witnesses knowing that Mr. Brooks had made a fresh will, Mr. Wethered's partner, his clerk, or one of the confidential servants in the house. Therefore *a* will must be discovered after the old man's death.

"Now, Murray Brooks was not an expert forger; it takes years of training to become that. A forged will executed by himself would be sure to be found out—yes, that's it, sure to be found out. The forgery will be palpable—let it be palpable, and then it will be found out, branded as such, and the original will of 1891, so favorable to the young blackguard's interests, would be held as valid. Was it devilry or merely additional caution which prompted Murray to pen that forged will so glaringly in Percival's favor? It is impossible to say.

"Anyhow, it was the cleverest touch in that marvelously devised crime. To plan that evil deed was great, to execute it was easy enough. He had several hours' leisure in which to do it. Then at night it was simplicity itself to slip the document under the dead man's pillow. Sacrilege causes no shudder to such natures as Murray Brooks's. The rest of the drama you know already—"

"But Percival Brooks?"

"The jury returned a verdict of 'Not guilty.' There was no evidence against him."

"But the money? Surely the scoundrel does not have the enjoyment of it still?"

"No; he enjoyed it for a time, but he died about three months ago, and forgot to take the precaution of making a will, so his brother Percival has got the business after all. If you ever go to Dublin, I should order some of Brooks's bacon if I were you. It is very good."

❧ | Carolyn Wells

"Clue or Clew—In detective stories any pertinent information which the detective has which helps him solve a crime. The better the plot is, the more elusive the clue is to the reader."

This definition of the clue appears in the authoritative volume on the detective story called *Who Done It*. But the great practitioners of the detective story know that half of the fun of the game is the building up of false clues, of feints in first one direction and parries in another.

Carolyn Wells was one of the most popular American writers of the detective story. A prolific writer in many fields, she wrote more than 170 books. Her very first, published in 1909, was appropriately enough entitled *The Clue*. In it she introduced a detective called Fleming Stone, who appeared in roughly eighty books. This early story by Miss Wells is not a Fleming Stone story, but one in which her delightful touch of parody is apparent. Miss Wells was one of the twentieth century's most brilliant historians of parody and satire. Her book *A Nonsense Anthology* (1902) is still an important reference.

The accomplishments of this gallant woman writer and dedicated craftsman were particularly rewarding, because she was almost totally deaf from the age of six as a result of a severe case of the then virulent scarlet fever.

Christabel's Crystal

Of all the unexpected pleasures that have come into my life, I think perhaps the greatest was when Christabel Farland asked me to be bridesmaid at her wedding.

I always had liked Christabel at college, and though we hadn't seen much of each other since we were graduated, I still had a strong feeling of friendship for her, and besides that I was glad to be one of the merry house party gathered at Farland Hall for the wedding festivities.

I arrived the afternoon before the wedding-day, and found the family and guests drinking tea in the library. Two other bridesmaids were there, Alice Fordham and Janet White, with both of whom I was slightly acquainted. The men, however, except Christabel's brother Fred, were strangers to me, and were introduced as Mr. Richmond, who was to be an usher; Herbert Gay, a neighbor, who chanced to be calling; and Mr. Wayne, the tutor of Christabel's younger brother Harold. Mrs. Farland was there too, and her welcoming words to me were as sweet and cordial as Christabel's.

The party was in frivolous mood, and as the jests and laughter grew more hilarious, Mrs. Farland declared that she would take the bride-elect away to her room for a quiet rest, lest she should not appear at her best the next day.

"Come with me, Elinor," said Christabel to me, "and I will show you my wedding-gifts."

Together we went to the room set apart for the purpose, and on many white-draped tables I saw displayed the gorgeous profusion of silver, glass and bric-à-brac that are one of the chief component parts of a wedding of to-day.

I had gone entirely through my vocabulary of ecstatic adjectives and was beginning over again, when we came to a small table which held only one wedding-gift.

"That is the gem of the whole collection," said Christabel, with a happy smile, "not only because Laurence gave it to me, but because of its intrinsic perfection and rarity."

I looked at the bridegroom's gift in some surprise. Instead of the conventional diamond sunburst or heart-shaped brooch, I saw a crystal ball as large as a fair-sized orange.

I knew of Christabel's fondness for Japanese crystals and that she had a number of small ones of varying qualities; but this magnificent specimen fairly took my breath away. It was poised on the top of one of those wavecrests, which the artisans seem to think appropriately interpreted in wrought-iron. Now, I haven't the same subtle sympathy with crystals that Christabel always has had; but still this great, perfect, limpid sphere affected me strangely. I glanced at it at first with a calm interest; but as I continued to look I became fascinated, and soon found myself obliged (if I may use the expression) to tear my eyes away.

Christabel watched me curiously. "Do you love it too?" she said, and then she turned her eyes to the crystal with a rapt and rapturous gaze that made her appear lovelier than ever. "Wasn't it dear of Laurence?" she said. "He wanted to give me jewels of course; but I told him that I would rather have this big crystal than the Koh-i-nur. I have six others, you know; but the largest of them hasn't one-third the diameter of this."

"It is wonderful," I said, "and I am glad you have it. I must own it frightens me a little."

"That is because of its perfection," said Christabel simply. "Absolute flawless perfection always is awesome. And when it is combined with perfect, faultless beauty, it is the ultimate perfection of a material thing."

"But I thought you liked crystals because of their weird supernatural influence over you," I said.

"That is an effect, not a cause," Christabel replied. "Ultimate perfection is so rare in our experiences that its existence perforce produces consequences so rare as to be dubbed weird and supernatural. But I must not gaze at my crystal longer now, or I shall forget that it is my wedding-day. I'm not going to look at it again until after I return from my wedding-trip; and then, as I tell Laurence, he will have to share my affection with his wedding-gift to me."

Christabel gave the crystal a long parting look, and then ran away to don her wedding-gown. "Elinor," she called over her shoulder, as she neared her own door, "I'll leave my crystal in your special care. See that nothing happens to it while I'm away."

"Trust me!" I called back gaily, and then went in search of my sister bridesmaids.

The morning after the wedding began rather later than most mornings. But at last we all were seated at the breakfast-table and enthusiastically discussing the events of the night before. It seemed strange to be there without Christabel, and Mrs. Farland said that I must stay until the bridal pair returned, for she couldn't get along without a daughter of some sort.

This remark made me look anywhere rather than at Fred Farland, and so I chanced to catch Harold's eye. But the boy gave me such an intelligent, mischievous smile that I actually blushed and was covered with confusion.

Just at that moment Katy the parlor-maid came into the dining-room, and with an anxious expression on her face said:

"Mrs. Farland, do you know anything about Miss Christabel's glass ball? It isn't in the present-room."

"No," said Mrs. Farland; "but I suppose Mr. Haley put it in the safe with the silver and jewelry."

"I don't think so, ma'am; for he asked me was he to take any of the cut glass, and I told him you had said only the silver and gold, ma'am."

"But that crystal isn't cut glass, Katy; and it's more valuable than all Miss Christabel's silver gifts put together."

"Oh, my! is it, ma'am? Well, then, won't you please see if it's all right, for I'm worried about it."

I wish I could describe my feelings at this moment. Have you ever been in imminent danger of a fearful catastrophe of any kind, and while with all your heart and soul you hoped it might be averted, yet there was one little, tiny, hidden impulse of your mind that craved the excitement of the disaster? Perhaps it is only an ignoble nature that can have this experience, or there may be a partial excuse for me in the fact that I am afflicted with what sometimes is called the "detective instinct." I say afflicted, for I well know that anyone else who has this particular mental bias will agree with me that it causes far more annoyance than satisfaction.

Why, one morning when I met Mrs. Van Allen in the market, I said: "It's too bad your waitress had to go out of town to attend the funeral of a near relative, when you were expecting company to luncheon." And she was as angry as could be, and called me an impertinent busy-body.

But I just had deduced it all from her glove. You see, she had on one brand-new black-kid glove, and the other, though crumpled up in her hand, I could see never had been on at all. So I knew that she wouldn't start to market early in the morning with such gloves if she had any sort of half-worn black ones at all.

And I knew that she had given away her next-best pair recently—it must have been the night before, or she would have tried them on sooner; and as her cook is an enormous woman, I was sure that she had given them to her waitress. And why would she, unless the maid was going away in great haste? And what would require such a condition of things except a sudden call to a funeral? And it must have been out of town, or she would have waited until morning, and then she could have bought black gloves for herself. And it must have been a near relative to make the case so urgent. And I knew that Mrs. Van Allen expected luncheon guests, because her fingers were stained from paring apples; and why would she pare her own apples so early in the morning except to assist the cook in some hurried preparations? Why, it was all as plain as could be, and every bit true; but Mrs. Van Allen wouldn't believe my explanation, and to this day she thinks I made my discoveries by gossiping with her servants.

Perhaps all this will help you to understand why I felt a sort of nervous exhilaration that had in it an element of secret pleasure, when we learned that Christabel's crystal really was missing.

Mr. Haley, who was a policeman, had remained in the present-room during all of the hours devoted to the wedding celebration, and after the guests had gone he had packed up the silver, gold and jewels and put them away in the family safe, which stood in a small dressing-room between Mrs. Farland's bedroom and Fred's. He had worn civilian's dress during the evening, and few if any of the guests knew that he was guarding the valuable gifts. The mistake had been in not telling him explicitly to care for the crystal as the most valuable gem of all; but this point had been overlooked, and the ignorant officer had assumed that it was merely a piece of cut glass, of no more value than any of the carafes or decanters. When told that the ball's intrinsic value was many thousands of dollars, and that it would be next to impossible to duplicate it at any price, his amazement was unbounded, and he appeared extremely grave.

"You ought to have told me," he said. "Sure, it's a case for the chief now!" Haley had been hastily telephoned for to come to Farland Hall and tell his story, and now he telephoned for the chief of police and a detective.

I felt a thrill of delight at this, for I always had longed to see a real detective in the act of detecting.

Of course everybody was greatly excited, and I just gave myself up to the enjoyment of the situation, when suddenly I remembered that Christabel had said that she would leave her crystal in my charge, and that in a way I was responsible for its safety. This changed my whole attitude, and I realized that, instead of being an idly curious observer, I must put all my detective instinct to work immediately and use every endeavor to recover the lost crystal.

First, I flew to my own room and sat down for a few moments to collect my thoughts and lay my plans. Of course, as the windows of the present-room were found in the morning fastened as they were left the night before, the theft must have been committed by someone in the house. Naturally it was not one of the family or the guests of the house. As to the servants, they all were honest and trustworthy—I had Mrs. Farland's word for that. There was no reason to suspect the policeman, and thus my process of elimination brought me to Mr. Wayne, Harold's tutor.

Of course it must have been the tutor. In nine-tenths of all the detective stories I ever have read the criminal proved to be a tutor or secretary or some sort of gentlemanly dependent of the family; and now I had come upon a detective story in real life, and here was the regulation criminal ready to fit right into it. It was the tutor of course; but I should be discreet and not name him until I had collected some undeniable evidence.

Next, I went down to the present-room to search for clues.

The detective had not arrived yet, and I was glad to be first on the ground, for I remembered how much importance Sherlock Holmes always attached to the first search. I didn't really expect that the tutor had left shreds of his clothing clinging to the table-legs, or anything absurd like that; but I fully expected to find a clue of some sort. I hoped that it wouldn't be cigar ashes; for though detectives in fiction always can tell the name and price of a cigar from a bit of ash, yet I'm so ignorant about such things that all ashes are alike to me.

I hunted carefully all over the floor; but I couldn't find a thing that seemed the least bit like a clue, except a faded white carnation. Of course that wasn't an unusual thing to find, the day after a wedding; but it surprised me some, because it was the very flower I had given to Fred Farland the night before, and he had worn it in his buttonhole. I recognized it perfectly, for it was wired, and I had twisted it a certain way when I adjusted it for him.

This didn't seem like strong evidence against the tutor; but it was convincing to me, for if Mr. Wayne was villain enough to steal Christabel's crystal, he was wicked enough to manage to get Fred's boutonnière and leave it in the room, hoping thereby to incriminate Fred. So fearful was I that this trick might make trouble for Fred that I said nothing about the carnation; for I knew that it was in Fred's coat when he said good-night, and then we all went directly to our rooms. When the detective came he examined the room, and I know that he didn't find anything in the way of evidence; but he tried to appear as if he had, and he frowned and jotted down notes in a book after the most approved fashion.

Then he called in everybody who had been in the house over night and questioned each one. I could see at once that his questions to the family and guests were purely perfunctory, and that he too had his suspicions of the tutor.

Finally, it was Mr. Wayne's turn. He always was a nervous little man, and now he seemed terribly flustered. The detective was gentle with him, and in order to set him more at ease began to converse generally on crystals. He asked Mr. Wayne if he had traveled much, if he ever had been to Japan, and if he knew much about the making and polishing of crystal balls.

The tutor fidgeted around a good deal and seemed disinclined to look the detective in the eye; but he replied that he never had been to Japan, and that he never had heard of a Japanese rock crystal until he had seen Miss Farland's wedding-gift; and that even then he had no idea of its great value until since its disappearance he had heard its price named.

This sounded well; but his manner was so embarrassed, and he had such an effect of a guilty man, that I felt sure my intuitions were correct and that he himself was the thief.

The detective seemed to think so too, for he said at last: "Mr. Wayne, your words seem to indicate your innocence; but your attitudes do not. Unless you can explain why you are so agitated and apparently afraid, I shall be forced to the conclusion that you know more about this than you have admitted."

Then Mr. Wayne said: "Must I tell all I know about it, sir?"

"Certainly," said the detective.

"Then," said Mr. Wayne, "I shall have to state that when I left my room late last night to get a glass of water from the ice-pitcher, which always stands on the hall-table, I saw Mr. Fred Farland just going into the sitting-room, or present-room, as it has been called for the last few days."

There was a dead silence. This, then, was why Mr. Wayne had acted so embarrassed; this was the explanation of my finding the white carnation there; and I think the detective thought that the sudden turn affairs had taken incriminated Fred Farland.

I didn't think so at all. The idea of Fred's stealing his own sister's wedding-gift was too preposterous to be considered for a moment.

"Were you in the room late at night, Mr. Farland?" asked the detective.

"I was," said Fred.

"Why didn't you tell me this before?"

"You didn't ask me, and as I didn't take the crystal I saw no reason for referring to the fact that I was in the room."

"Why did you go there?"

"I went," said Fred coolly, "with the intention of taking the crystal and hiding it, as a practical joke on Christabel."

"Why did you not do so?"

"Because the ball wasn't there. I didn't think then that it had been stolen, but that it had been put away safely with the other valuables. Since this is not so, and the crystal is missing, we all must get to work and find it somehow before my sister returns."

The tutor seemed like a new man after Fred had spoken. His face cleared, and he appeared intelligent, alert and entirely at his ease. "Let me help," he said. "Pray command my services in any way you choose."

But the detective didn't seem so reassured by Fred's statements. Indeed, I believe he really thought that Christabel's brother was guilty of theft.

But I believed implicitly every word Fred had uttered and, begging him to come with me, I led the way again to the sitting-room. Mr. Wayne and Janet White came too, and the four of us scrutinized the floor, walls and furniture of the room over and over again. "There's one thing certain," I said thoughtfully: "The crystal was taken either by someone in the house or someone out of it. We've been confining our suspicions to those inside. Why not a real burglar?"

"But the windows are fastened on the inside," said Janet.

"I know it," I replied. "But if a burglar could slip a catch with a thin-bladed knife—and they often do—then he could slip it back again with the same knife and so divert suspicion."

"Bravo, Miss Frost!" said Mr. Wayne, with an admiring glance at me. "You have the true detective instinct. I'll go outside and see if there are any traces."

A moment later he was on the veranda and excitedly motioning us to raise the window. Fred pushed back the catch and opened the long French window that opened on the front veranda.

"I believe Miss Frost has discovered the mystery," said Mr. Wayne, and he pointed to numerous scratches on the sash-frame. The house had been painted recently, and it was seen easily that the fresh scratches were made by a thin knife-blade pushed between the sashes.

"By Jove!" cried Fred, "that's it, Elinor; and the canny fellow had wit enough to push the catch back in place after he was outside again."

I said nothing, for a moment. My thoughts were adjusting themselves quickly to the new situation from which I must make my deductions. I realized at once that I must give up my theory of the tutor, of course, and anyway I hadn't had a scrap of evidence against him except his fitness for the position. But, given the surety of burglars from outside, I knew just what to do: look for footprints, to be sure.

I glanced around for the light snow that always falls in detective stories just before the crime is committed, and is testified, usually by the village folk, to have stopped just at the crucial moment. But there wasn't a sign of snow or rain or even dew. The veranda showed no footprints, nor could the smooth lawn or flagged walks be expected to. I leaned against the veranda railing in despair, wondering what Sherlock Holmes would do in a provoking absence of footprints, when I saw in the flower-bed beneath several well-defined marks of a man's shoes.

"There you are, Fred!" I cried, and rushed excitedly down the steps.

They all followed, and, sure enough, in the soft earth of the wide flower-bed that surrounded the veranda were strong, clear prints of large masculine footgear.

"That clears us, girls," cried Janet gleefully, as she measured her daintily shod foot against the depressions.

"Don't touch them!" I cried. "Call Mr. Prout the detective."

Mr. Prout appeared, and politely hiding his chagrin at not having discovered these marks before I did, proceeded to examine them closely.

"You see," he said in a pompous and dictatorial way, "there are four prints pointing toward the house, and four pointing toward the street. Those pointing to the street are superimposed upon those leading to the house, hence we deduce that they were made by a burglar who crossed the flower-bed, climbed the veranda, stepped over the rail and entered at the window. He then returned the same way, leaving these last footprints above the others."

As all this was so palpably evident from the facts of the case, I was not impressed much by the subtlety of his deductions and asked him what he gathered from the shape of the prints.

He looked at the well-defined prints intently. "They are of a medium size," he announced at last, "and I should say that they were made by a man of average height and weight, who had a normal-sized foot."

Well, if that wasn't disappointing! I thought of course that he would tell the man's occupation and social status, even if he didn't say that he was left-handed or that he stuttered, which is the kind of thing detectives in fiction always discover.

So I lost all interest in that Prout man, and began to do a little deducing on my own account. Although I felt sure, as we all did, that the thief was a burglar from outside, yet I couldn't measure the shoes of an absent and unidentified burglar, and somehow I felt an uncontrollable impulse to measure shoes.

Without consulting anybody, I found a tape-measure and carefully measured the footprints. Then I went through the house and measured all the men's shoes I could find, from the stable-boy's up to Fred's.

It's an astonishing fact, but nearly all of them fitted the measurements of the prints on the flower-bed. Men's feet are so nearly universal in size, or rather their shoes are, and too, what with extension soles and queer-shaped lasts, you can't tell anything about the size or style of a man from his footprints.

So I gave up deducing and went to talk to Fred Farland.

"Fred," I said simply, "did you take Christabel's crystal?"

"No," he answered with equal simplicity, and he looked me in the eyes so squarely and honestly that I knew he spoke the truth.

"Who did?" I next inquired.

"It was a professional burglar," said Fred, "and a mighty cute one; but I'm going to track him and get that crystal back before Christabel comes home."

"Let me help!" I cried eagerly. "I've got the true detective instinct, and I know I can do something."

"You?" said Fred incredulously. "No, you can't help; but I don't mind telling you my plan. You see I expect Lord Hammerton down to make me a visit. He's a jolly young English chap that I chummed with in London. Now, he's a first-rate amateur detective, and though I didn't expect him till next month, he's in New York, and I've no doubt that he'd be willing to come right off. No one will know he's doing any detecting; and I'll wager he'll lay his hands on that ball in less than a week."

"Lovely!" I exclaimed. "And I'll be here to see him do it!"

"Yes, the mater says you're to stay a fortnight or more; but mind, this is our secret."

"Trust me," I said earnestly; "but let me help if I can, won't you?"

"You'll help most by not interfering," declared Fred, and though it didn't altogether suit me, I resolved to help that way rather than not at all.

A few days later Lord Hammerton came. He was not in any way an imposing-looking man. Indeed, he was a typical Englishman of the Lord Cholmondeley type, and drawled and used a monocle most effectively. The afternoon he came we told him all about the crystal. The talk turned to detective work and detective instinct. Lord Hammerton opined in his slow languid drawl that the true detective mind was not dependent upon instinct, but was a nicely adjusted mentality that was quick to see the cause back of an effect.

Herbert Gay said that while this doubtless was so, yet it was an even chance whether the cause so skilfully deduced was the true one.

"Quite so," agreed Lord Hammerton amiably, "and that is why the detective in real life fails so often. He deduces properly the logical facts from the evidence before him; but real life and real events are so illogical that his deductions, though true theoretically, are false from mere force of circumstances."

"And that is why," I said, "detectives in story-books always deduce rightly, because the obliging author makes the literal facts coincide with the theoretical ones."

Lord Hammerton put up his monocle and favored me with a truly British stare. "It is unusual," he remarked slowly, "to find such a clear comprehension of this subject in a feminine mind."

They all laughed at this; but I went on: "It is easy enough to make the spectacular detective of fiction show marvelous penetration and logical deduction when the antecedent circumstances are arranged carefully to prove it all; but place even Sherlock Holmes face to face with a total stranger, and I, for one, don't believe that he could tell anything definite about him."

"Oh, come now! I can't agree to that," said Lord Hammerton, more interestedly than he had spoken before. "I believe there is much in the detective instinct besides the exotic and the artificial. There is a substantial basis of divination built on minute observation, and which I have picked up in some measure myself."

"Let us test that statement," cried Herbert Gay. "Here comes Mr. Wayne, Harold's tutor. Lord Hammerton never has seen him, and before Wayne even speaks let Lord Hammerton tell us some detail, which he divines by observation."

All agreed to this, and a few minutes later Mr. Wayne came up. We laughingly explained the situation to him and asked him to have himself deduced.

Lord Hammerton looked at Arthur Wayne for a few minutes, and then said, still in his deliberate drawl: "You have lived in Japan for the past seven years, in Government service in the interior, and only recently have returned."

A sudden silence fell upon us all—not so much because Lord Hammerton made deductions from no apparent evidence, but because we all knew Mr. Wayne had told Detective Prout that he never had been in Japan.

Fred Farland recovered himself first, and said: "Now that you've astonished us with your results, tell us how you attained them."

"It is simple enough," said Lord Hammerton, looking at young Wayne, who had turned deathly white. "It is simple enough, sir. The breast-pocket on the outside of your coat is on the right-hand side. Now it never is put there. Your coat is a good one—Poole, or some London tailor of that class. He never made a coat with an outer breast-pocket on the right side. You have had the coat turned—thus the original left-hand pocket appears now on the right side.

"Looking at you, I see that you have not the constitution which could recover from an acute attack of poverty. If you had it turned from want, you would not have your present effect of comfortable circumstances. Now, you must have had it turned because you were in a country where tailoring is not frequent, but sewing and delicate manipulation easy to find. India? You are not bronzed. China? The same. Japan? Probable; but not treaty ports—there are plenty of tailors there. Hence, the interior of Japan.

"Long residence, to make it incumbent on you to get the coat turned, means Government service, because unattached foreigners are allowed only as tourists. Then the cut of the coat is not so very old, and as contracts run seven or fourteen years with the Japanese, I repeat that you probably resided seven years in the interior of Japan, possibly as an irrigation engineer."

I felt sorry then for poor Mr. Wayne. Lord Hammerton's deductions were absolutely true, and coming upon the young man so suddenly he made no attempt to refute them.

And so as he had been so long in Japan, and must have been familiar with rock crystals for years, Fred questioned him sternly in reference to his false statements.

Then he broke down completely and confessed that he had taken Christabel's crystal because it had fascinated him.

He declared that he had a morbid craving for crystals; that he had crept down to the present-room late that night, merely to look at the wonderful, beautiful ball; that it had so possessed him that he carried it to his room to gaze at for a while, intending to return with it after an hour or so. When he returned he saw Fred Farland, and dared not carry out his plan.

"And the footprints?" I asked eagerly.

"I made them myself," he explained with a dogged shamefacedness. "I did have a moment of temptation to keep the crystal, and so tried to make you think that a burglar had taken it; but the purity and beauty of the ball itself so reproached me that I tried to return it. I didn't do so then, and since—"

"Since?" urged Fred, not unkindly.

"Well, I've been torn between fear and the desire to keep the ball. You will find it in my trunk. Here is the key."

There was a certain dignity about the young man that made him seem unlike a criminal, or even a wrong-doer.

As for me, I entirely appreciated the fact that he was hypnotized by the crystal and in a way was not responsible. I don't believe that man would steal anything else in the world.

Somehow the others agreed with me, and as they had recovered the ball, they took no steps to prosecute Mr. Wayne.

He went away at once, still in that dazed, uncertain condition. We never saw him again; but I hope for his own sake that he never was subjected to such a temptation.

Just before he left, I said to him out of sheer curiosity: "Please explain one point, Mr. Wayne. Since you opened and closed that window purposely to mislead us, since you made those footprints in the flower-bed for the same reason, and since to do it you must have gone out and then come back, why were the outgoing footprints made over the incoming ones?"

"I walked backward on purpose," said Mr. Wayne simply.

❧ | Agatha Christie

"I bet you can't write a good detective story." Spurred on years ago by this challenge from her sister, the writer we now know as Dame Agatha Christie celebrated her eightieth birthday with the publication of her eightieth book. Second in popularity only to the works of William Shakespeare, translations of her work appear all over the world.

Her detective Hercule Poirot was created from Dame Agatha's acquaintance with a group of Belgian refugees in England during World War I. Her books ushered in what was to be called the golden age of the detective story. This was an age, everlastingly debating the who, why, and how, that was to make the ground rules of detective story writing, rules that Dame Agatha often chose to ignore. In doing so, she created the most famous detective since Sherlock Holmes.

Howard Haycroft, the foremost authority on the detective story, in celebrating the hundredth anniversary of the detective story in 1941, singled out Poirot for special praise:

"Happily, Poirot richly merited the attention he received. For when he is at the top of his form few fictional sleuths can surpass the amazing Belgian—with his waxed mustaches and egg-shaped head, his inflated confidence in the infallibility of his 'little grey cells,' his murderous attacks on the English language—either for individuality or ingenuity. His methods, as the mention of the seldom-forgotten 'cells' implies, are imaginative, rather than routine. Not for Poirot the fingerprint or the cigar ash. His picturesque refusal to go Holmes-like on all fours in pursuit of the clues is classic in literature."

Understandably reluctant to talk about her work, Dame Agatha admitted, "I don't enjoy writing detective stories. I enjoy thinking of a detective story, planning, but when the time comes to write it, it is like going to work every day, like having a job." And, said Dame Agatha, her inspirations often came in a delightful fashion—while she was sitting in the bathtub, munching apples.

The Plymouth Express

Alec Simpson, R.N., stepped from the platform at Newton Abbot into a first-class compartment of the Plymouth Express. A porter followed him with a heavy suitcase. He was about to swing it up to the rack, but the young sailor stopped him.

"No—leave it on the seat. I'll put it up later. Here you are."

"Thank you, sir." The porter, generously tipped, withdrew.

Doors banged; a stentorian voice shouted: "Plymouth only. Change for Torquay. Plymouth next stop." Then a whistle blew, and the train drew slowly out of the station.

Lieutenant Simpson had the carriage to himself. The December air was chilly, and he pulled up the window. Then he sniffed vaguely, and frowned. What a smell there was! Reminded him of that time in hospital, and the operation on his leg. Yes, chloroform; that was it!

He let the window down again, changing his seat to one with its back to the engine. He pulled a pipe out of his pocket and lit it. For a time he sat inactive, looking out into the night and smoking.

At last he roused himself and, opening the suitcase, took out some papers and magazines, then closed the suitcase again and endeavored to shove it under the opposite seat—without success. Some hidden obstacle resisted it. He shoved harder with rising impatience, but it still stuck out halfway into the carriage.

"Why the devil won't it go in?" he muttered and, hauling it

out completely, he stooped down and peered under the seat. . . .

A moment later a cry rang out into the night, and the great train came to an unwilling halt in obedience to the imperative jerking of the communication-cord.

"*Mon ami,*" said Poirot, "you have, I know, been deeply interested in this mystery of the Plymouth Express. Read this."

I picked up the note he flicked across the table to me. It was brief and to the point.

Dear Sir:
I shall be obliged if you will call upon me at your earliest convenience.
Yours faithfully,
Ebenezer Halliday.

The connection was not clear to my mind, and I looked inquiringly at Poirot.

For answer he took up the newspaper and read aloud:

" 'A sensational discovery was made last night. A young naval officer returning to Plymouth found under the seat of his compartment the body of a woman, stabbed through the heart. The officer at once pulled the communication-cord, and the train was brought to a standstill. The woman, who was about thirty years of age, and richly dressed, has not yet been identified.'

"And later we have this: 'The woman found dead in the Plymouth Express has been identified as the Honorable Mrs. Rupert Carrington.' You see now, my friend? Or if you do not, I will add this—Mrs. Rupert Carrington was, before her marriage, Flossie Halliday, daughter of old man Halliday, the steel king of America."

"And he has sent for you? Splendid!"

"I did him a little service in the past—an affair of bearer bonds. And also, when I was in Paris for a royal visit, I had Mademoiselle Flossie pointed out to me. *La jolie petite pension-*

naire! She had the *jolie dot* too! It caused trouble. She nearly made a bad affair."

"How was that?"

"A certain Count de la Rochefour. *Un bien mauvais sujet!* A bad hat, as you would say. An adventurer pure and simple, who knew how to appeal to a romantic young girl. Luckily her father got wind of it in time. He took her back to America in haste. I heard of her marriage some years later, but I know nothing of her husband."

"H'm," I said. "The Honorable Rupert Carrington is no beauty, by all accounts. He'd pretty well run through his own money on the turf, and I should imagine old man Halliday's dollars came along in the nick of time. I should say that for a good-looking, well-mannered, utterly unscrupulous young scoundrel, it would be hard to find his match!"

"Ah, the poor little lady! *Elle n'est pas bien tombée!*"

"I fancy he made it pretty obvious at once that it was her money, and not she, that had attracted him. I believe they drifted apart almost at once. I have heard rumors lately that there was to be a definite legal separation."

"Old man Halliday is no fool. He would tie up her money pretty tight."

"I dare say. Anyway, I know as a fact that the Honorable Rupert is said to be extremely hard up."

"Ah-ha! I wonder—"

"You wonder what?"

"My good friend, do not jump down my throat like that. You are interested, I see. Supposing you accompany me to see Mr. Halliday. There is a taxi stand at the corner."

A few minutes sufficed to whirl us to the superb house in Park Lane rented by the American magnate. We were shown into the library, and almost immediately we were joined by a large, stout man, with piercing eyes and an aggressive chin.

"M. Poirot?" said Mr. Halliday. "I guess I don't need to tell you what I want you for. You've read the papers, and I'm never one to let the grass grow under my feet. I happened to hear you were in London, and I remembered the good work you did over those bonds. Never forget a name. I've got the pick of Scotland Yard, but I'll have my own man as well. Money no object. All the dollars were made for my little girl—and now she's gone, I'll spend my last cent to catch the scoundrel that did it! See? So it's up to you to deliver the goods."

Poirot bowed.

"I accept, monsieur, all the more willingly that I saw your daughter in Paris several times. And now I will ask you to tell me the circumstances of her journey to Plymouth and any other details that seem to you to bear upon the case."

"Well, to begin with," responded Halliday, "she wasn't going to Plymouth. She was going to join a house-party at Avonmead Court, the Duchess of Swansea's place. She left London by the twelve-fourteen from Paddington, arriving at Bristol (where she had to change) at two-fifty. The principal Plymouth expresses, of course, run via Westbury, and do not go near Bristol at all. The twelve-fourteen does a nonstop run to Bristol, afterward stopping at Weston, Taunton, Exeter and Newton Abbot. My daughter traveled alone in her carriage, which was reserved as far as Bristol, her maid being in a third-class carriage in the next coach."

Poirot nodded, and Mr. Halliday went on: "The party at Avonmead Court was to be a very gay one, with several balls, and in consequence my daughter had with her nearly all her jewels—amounting in value, perhaps, to about a hundred thousand dollars."

"*Un moment*," interrupted Poirot. "Who had charge of the jewels? Your daughter, or the maid?"

"My daughter always took charge of them herself, carrying them in a small blue morocco case."

"Continue, monsieur."

"At Bristol the maid, Jane Mason, collected her mistress' dressing-bag and wraps, which were with her, and came to the door of Flossie's compartment. To her intense surprise, my daughter told her that she was not getting out at Bristol, but was going on farther. She directed Mason to get out the luggage and put it in the cloak-room. She could have tea in the refreshment-room, but she was to wait at the station for her mistress, who would return to Bristol by an up-train in the course of the afternoon. The maid, although very much astonished, did as she was told. She put the luggage in the cloak-room and had some tea. But up-train after up-train came in, and her mistress did not appear. After the arrival of the last train, she left the luggage where it was, and went to a hotel near the station for the night. This morning she read of the tragedy, and returned to town by the first available train."

"Is there nothing to account for your daughter's sudden change of plan?"

"Well, there is this: According to Jane Mason, at Bristol, Flossie was no longer alone in her carriage. There was a man in it who stood looking out of the farther window so that she could not see his face."

"The train was a corridor one, of course?"

"Yes."

"Which side was the corridor?"

"On the platform side. My daughter was standing in the corridor as she talked to Mason."

"And there is no doubt in your mind—excuse me!" He got up, and carefully straightened the inkstand which was a little askew. *"Je vous demande pardon,"* he continued, reseating himself. "It affects my nerves to see anything crooked. Strange, is it not? I was saying, monsieur, that there is no doubt in your mind, as to this probably unexpected meeting being the cause of your daughter's sudden change of plan?"

"It seems the only reasonable supposition."

"You have no idea as to who the gentleman in question might be?"

The millionaire hesitated for a moment, and then replied: "No—I do not know at all."

"Now—as to the discovery of the body?"

"It was discovered by a young naval officer who at once gave the alarm. There was a doctor on the train. He examined the body. She had been first chloroformed, and then stabbed. He gave it as his opinion that she had been dead about four hours, so it must have been done not long after leaving Bristol—probably between there and Weston, possibly between Weston and Taunton."

"And the jewel-case?"

"The jewel-case, M. Poirot, was missing."

"One thing more, monsieur. Your daughter's fortune—to whom does it pass at her death?"

"Flossie made a will soon after her marriage, leaving everything to her husband." He hesitated for a minute, and then went on: "I may as well tell you, Monsieur Poirot, that I regard my son-in-law as an unprincipled scoundrel, and that, by my advice, my daughter was on the eve of freeing herself from him by legal means—no difficult matter. I settled her money upon her in such a way that he could not touch it during her lifetime, but although they have lived entirely apart for some years, she has frequently acceded to his demands for money, rather than face an open scandal. However, I was determined to put an end to this. At last Flossie agreed, and my lawyers were instructed to take proceedings."

"And where is Monsieur Carrington?"

"In town. I believe he was away in the country yesterday, but he returned last night."

Poirot considered a little while. Then he said: "I think that is all, monsieur."

"You would like to see the maid, Jane Mason?"

"If you please."

Halliday rang the bell, and gave a short order to the footman.

A few minutes later Jane Mason entered the room, a respectable, hard-featured woman, as emotionless in the face of tragedy as only a good servant can be.

"You will permit me to put a few questions? Your mistress, she was quite as usual before starting yesterday morning? Not excited or flurried?"

"Oh, no sir!"

"But at Bristol she was quite different?"

"Yes sir, regular upset—so nervous she didn't seem to know what she was saying."

"What did she say exactly?"

"Well, sir, as near as I can remember, she said: 'Mason, I've got to alter my plans. Something has happened—I mean, I'm not getting out here after all. I must go on. Get out the luggage and put it in the cloak-room; then have some tea, and wait for me in the station.'

" 'Wait for you here, ma'am?' I asked.

" 'Yes, yes. Don't leave the station. I shall return by a later train. I don't know when. It mayn't be until quite late.'

" 'Very well, ma'am,' I says. It wasn't my place to ask questions, but I thought it very strange."

"It was unlike your mistress, eh?"

"Very unlike her, sir."

"What do you think?"

"Well, sir, I thought it was to do with the gentleman in the carriage. She didn't speak to him, but she turned round once or twice as though to ask him if she was doing right."

"But you didn't see the gentleman's face?"

"No sir; he stood with his back to me all the time."

"Can you describe him at all?"

"He had on a light fawn overcoat, and a traveling-cap. He was tall and slender, like, and the back of his head was dark."

"You didn't know him?"

"Oh, no, I don't think so, sir."

"It was not your master, Mr. Carrington, by any chance?"

Mason looked rather startled.

"Oh! I don't think so, sir!"

"But you are not *sure*?"

"It was about the master's build, sir—but I never thought of it being him. We so seldom saw him. . . . I couldn't say it *wasn't* him!"

Poirot picked up a pin from the carpet, and frowned at it severely; then he continued: "Would it be possible for the man to have entered the train at Bristol before you reached the carriage?"

Mason considered.

"Yes sir, I think it would. My compartment was very crowded, and it was some minutes before I could get out—and then there was a very large crowd on the platform, and that delayed me too. But he'd only have had a minute or two to speak to the mistress, that way. I took it for granted that he'd come along the corridor."

"That is more probable, certainly."

He paused, still frowning.

"You know how the mistress was dressed, sir?"

"The papers give a few details, but I would like you to confirm them."

"She was wearing a white fox fur toque, sir, with a white

spotted veil, and a blue frieze coat and skirt—the shade of blue they call electric."

"H'm, rather striking."

"Yes," remarked Mr. Halliday. "Inspector Japp is in hopes that that may help us to fix the spot where the crime took place. Anyone who saw her would remember her."

"*Précisément!*—Thank you, mademoiselle."

The maid left the room.

"Well!" Poirot got up briskly. "That is all I can do here—except, monsieur, that I would ask you to tell me everything—but *everything*!"

"I have done so."

"You are sure?"

"Absolutely."

"Then there is nothing more to be said. I must decline the case."

"Why?"

"Because you have not been frank with me."

"I assure you—"

"No, you're keeping something back."

There was a moment's pause, and then Halliday drew a paper from his pocket and handed it to my friend.

"I guess that's what you're after, Monsieur Poirot—though how you know about it fairly gets my goat!"

Poirot smiled, and unfolded the paper. It was a letter written in thin sloping handwriting. Poirot read it aloud.

" 'Chère Madame:

" 'It is with infinite pleasure that I look forward to the felicity of meeting you again. After your so amiable reply to my letter, I can hardly restrain my impatience. I have never forgotten those days in Paris. It is most cruel that you should be leaving London tomorrow. However, before very long, and perhaps sooner than you think, I shall have the joy of beholding once more the lady whose image has ever reigned supreme in my heart.

" 'Believe, chère madame, all the assurances of my most devoted and unaltered sentiments—

" 'Armand de la Rochefour.' "

Poirot handed the letter back to Halliday with a bow.

"I fancy, monsieur, that you did not know that your daughter intended renewing her acquaintance with the Count de la Rochefour?"

"It came as a thunderbolt to me! I found this letter in my daughter's handbag. As you probably know, Monsieur Poirot, this so-called count is an adventurer of the worst type."

Poirot nodded.

"But I want to know how you knew of the existence of this letter?"

My friend smiled. "Monsieur, I did not. But to track footmarks and recognize cigarette-ash is not sufficient for a detective. He must also be a good psychologist! I knew that you disliked and mistrusted your son-in-law. He benefits by your daughter's death; the maid's description of the mysterious man bears a sufficient resemblance to him. Yet you are not keen on his track! Why? Surely because your suspicions lie in another direction. Therefore you were keeping something back."

"You're right, Monsieur Poirot. I was sure of Rupert's guilt until I found this letter. It unsettled me horribly."

"Yes. The Count says: 'Before very long, and perhaps sooner than you think.' Obviously he would not want to wait until you should get wind of his reappearance. Was it he who traveled down from London by the twelve-fourteen, and came along the corridor to your daughter's compartment? The Count de la Rochefour is also, if I remember rightly, tall and dark!"

The millionaire nodded.

"Well, monsieur, I will wish you good day. Scotland Yard, has, I presume, a list of the jewels?"

"Yes. I believe Inspector Japp is here now if you would like to see him."

Japp was an old friend of ours, and greeted Poirot with a sort of affectionate contempt.

"And how are you, monsieur? No bad feeling between us, though we *have* our different ways of looking at things. How are the 'little gray cells,' eh? Going strong?"

Poirot beamed upon him. "They function, my good Japp; assuredly they do!"

"Then that's all right. Think it was the Honorable Rupert, or a crook? We're keeping an eye on all the regular places, of course. We shall know if the shiners are disposed of, and of course whoever did it isn't going to keep them to admire their sparkle. Not likely! I'm trying to find out where Rupert Carrington was yesterday. Seems a bit of a mystery about it. I've got a man watching him."

"A great precaution, but perhaps a day late," suggested Poirot gently.

"You always will have your joke, Monsieur Poirot. Well, I'm off to Paddington. Bristol, Weston, Taunton, that's my beat. So long."

"You will come round and see me this evening, and tell me the result?"

"Sure thing, if I'm back."

"That good Inspector believes in matter in motion," murmured Poirot as our friend departed. "He travels; he measures footprints; he collects mud and cigarette-ash! He is extremely busy! He is zealous beyond words! And if I mentioned psychology to him, do you know what he would do, my friend?

He would smile! He would say to himself: 'Poor old Poirot! He ages! He grows senile!' Japp is the 'younger generation knocking on the door.' And *ma foi*! They are so busy knocking that they do not notice that the door is open!"

"And what are you going to do?"

"As we have *carte blanche*, I shall expend threepence in ringing up the Ritz—where you may have noticed our Count is staying. After that, as my feet are a little damp and I have sneezed twice, I shall return to my rooms and make myself a *tisano* over the spirit lamp!"

I did not see Poirot again until the following morning. I found him placidly finishing his breakfast.

"Well?" I inquired eagerly. "What has happened?"

"Nothing."

"But Japp?"

"I have not seen him."

"The Count?"

"He left the Ritz the day before yesterday."

"The day of the murder?"

"Yes."

"Then that settles it! Rupert Carrington is cleared."

"Because the Count de la Rochefour has left the Ritz? You go too fast, my friend."

"Anyway, he must be followed, arrested! But what could be his motive?"

"One hundred thousand dollars' worth of jewelry is a very good motive for anyone. No, the question to my mind is: why kill her? Why not simply steal the jewels? She would not prosecute."

"Why not?"

"Because she is a woman, *mon ami*. She once loved this man. Therefore she would suffer her loss in silence. And the Count, who is an extremely good psychologist where women are concerned,—hence his successes,—would know that perfectly well! On the other hand, if Rupert Carrington killed her, why take the jewels, which would incriminate him fatally?"

"As a blind."

"Perhaps you are right, my friend. Ah, here is Japp! I recognize his knock."

The Inspector was beaming good-humoredly.

"Morning, Poirot. Only just got back. I've done some good work! And you?"

"Me, I have arranged my ideas," replied Poirot placidly.

Japp laughed heartily.

"Old chap's getting on in years," he observed beneath his breath to me. "That won't do for us young folk," he said aloud.

"*Quel dommage?*" Poirot inquired.

"Well, do you want to hear what I've done?"

"You permit me to make a guess? You have found the knife with which the crime was committed, by the side of the line between Weston and Taunton, and you have interviewed the paper-boy who spoke to Mrs. Carrington at Weston!"

Japp's jaw fell. "How on earth did you know? Don't tell me it was those almighty 'little gray cells' of yours!"

"I am glad you admit for once that they are *all mighty*! Tell me, did she give the paper-boy a shilling for himself?"

"No, it was half a crown!" Japp had recovered his temper, and grinned. "Pretty extravagant, these rich Americans!"

"And in consequence the boy did not forget her?"

"Not he. Half-crowns don't come his way every day. She hailed him and bought two magazines. One had a picture of a girl in blue on the cover. 'That'll match me,' she said. Oh! He remembered her perfectly. Well, that was enough for me. By the doctor's evidence, the crime *must* have been committed before Taunton. I guessed they'd throw the knife away at once, and I walked down the line looking for it; and sure enough, there it was. I made inquiries at Taunton about our man, but of course it's a big station, and it wasn't likely they'd notice him. He probably got back to London by a later train."

Poirot nodded. "Very likely."

"But I found another bit of news when I got back. They're passing the jewels, all right! That large emerald was pawned last night—by one of the regular lot. Who do you think it was?"

"I don't know—except that he was a short man."

Japp stared. "Well, you're right there. He's short enough. It was Red Narky."

"Who is Red Narky?" I asked.

"A particularly sharp jewel-thief, sir. And not one to stick at murder. Usually works with a woman—Gracie Kidd; but she doesn't seem to be in it this time—unless she's got off to Holland with the rest of the swag."

"You've arrested Narky?"

"Sure thing. But mind you, it's the other man we want—the man who went down with Mrs. Carrington in the train. He was the one who planned the job, right enough. But Narky won't squeal on a pal."

I noticed that Poirot's eyes had become very green.

"I think," he said gently, "that I can find Narky's pal for you, all right."

"One of your little ideas, eh?" Japp eyed Poirot sharply. "Wonderful how you manage to deliver the goods sometimes, at your age and all. Devil's own luck, of course."

"Perhaps, perhaps," murmured my friend. "Hastings, my hat. And the brush. So! My galoshes, if it still rains! We must not undo the good work of that *tisano*. *Au revoir*, Japp!"

"Good luck to you, Poirot."

Poirot hailed the first taxi we met, and directed the driver to Park Lane.

When we drew up before Halliday's house, he skipped out nimbly, paid the driver and rang the bell. To the footman who opened the door he made a request in a low voice, and we were immediately taken upstairs. We went up to the top of the house, and were shown into a small neat bedroom.

Poirot's eyes roved round the room and fastened themselves on a small black trunk. He knelt in front of it, scrutinized the labels on it, and took a small twist of wire from his pocket.

"Ask Mr. Halliday if he will be so kind as to mount to me here," he said over his shoulder to the footman.

The man departed, and Poirot gently coaxed the lock of the trunk with a practiced hand. In a few minutes the lock gave, and he raised the lid of the trunk. Swiftly he began rummaging among the clothes it contained, flinging them out on the floor.

There was a heavy step on the stairs, and Halliday entered the room.

"What in hell are you doing here?" he demanded, staring.

"I was looking, monsieur, for *this*." Poirot withdrew from the trunk a coat and skirt of bright blue frieze, and a small toque of white fox fur.

"What are you doing with my trunk?" I turned to see that the maid, Jane Mason, had entered the room.

"If you will just shut the door, Hastings. Thank you. Yes, and stand with your back against it. Now, Mr. Halliday, let me introduce you to Gracie Kidd, otherwise Jane Mason, who will shortly rejoin her accomplice, Red Narky, under the kind escort of Inspector Japp."

Poirot waved a deprecating hand. "It was of the most simple!" He helped himself to more caviar.

"It was the maid's insistence on the clothes that her mistress was wearing that first struck me. Why was she so anxious that our attention should be directed to them? I reflected that we had only the maid's word for the mysterious man in the carriage at Bristol. As far as the doctor's evidence went, Mrs. Carrington might easily have been murdered *before* reaching Bristol. But if so, then the maid must be an accomplice. And if she were an accomplice, she would not wish this point to rest on her evidence alone. The clothes Mrs. Carrington was wearing were of a striking nature. A maid usually has a good deal of choice as to what her mistress shall wear. Now if, after Bristol, anyone saw a lady in a bright blue coat and skirt, and a fur toque, he will be quite ready to swear he has seen Mrs. Carrington.

"I began to reconstruct. The maid would provide herself with duplicate clothes. She and her accomplice chloroform and stab Mrs. Carrington between London and Bristol, probably taking advantage of a tunnel. Her body is rolled under the seat; and the maid takes her place. At Weston she must make herself noticed. How? In all probability, a newspaperboy will be selected. She will insure his remembering her by giving him a large tip. She also drew his attention to the color of her dress by a remark about one of the magazines. After leaving Weston, she throws the knife out of the window to mark the place where the crime presumably occurred, and changes her clothes, or buttons a long mackintosh over them. At Taunton she leaves the tram and returns to Bristol as soon as possible, where her accomplice has duly left the luggage in the cloak-room. He hands over the ticket and himself returns to London. She waits on the platform, carrying out her rôle, goes to a hotel for the night and returns to town in the morning, exactly as she said.

"When Japp returned from his expedition, he confirmed all my deductions. He also told me that a well-known crook was passing the jewels. I knew that whoever it was would be the exact opposite of the man Jane Mason described. When I heard that it was Red Narky, who always worked with Gracie Kidd— well, I knew just where to find her."

"And the Count?"

"The more I thought of it, the more I was convinced that he had nothing to do with it. That gentleman is much too careful of his own skin to risk murder. It would be out of keeping with his character."

"Well, Monsieur Poirot," said Halliday, "I owe you a big debt. And the check I write after lunch won't go near to settling it."

Poirot smiled modestly, and murmured to me: "The good Japp, he shall get the official credit, all right, but though he has got his Gracie Kidd, I think that I, as the Americans say, have got his goat!"

❧ | Dorothy L. Sayers

The entry in Who's Who runs: "WIMSEY, Peter Death Bredon (Lord), D.S.O., born 1890; second s. of Mortimer Gerald Bredon Wimsey, 15th Duke of Denver, and Honoria Lucasta, d. of Francis Delagardi of Bellingham Manor, Bucks. Educ. Eton College and Balliol College, Oxford. Served War of 1914-18 (Major, Rifle Brigade). Publications: 'Notes for Collectors of Incunabula,' 'The Murderer's Compendium,' etc. Recreations: Criminology, books, music, cricket. Clubs: Marlborough, Egoists'. Address: 110A Piccadilly, W.I.; Bredon Hall, Duke's Denver, Norfolk. Arms: Sable, three mice rampant argent; helmet: cat crouchant in natural colours; motto: As my wimsey takes me."

This imaginary insert into Who's Who is the work of one of the most individualistic and aristocratic of all detectives, Lord Peter Wimsey, the creation of Dorothy Leigh Sayers.

One of the greatest of the grande dames, some say the greatest, Dorothy Sayers, the daughter of a minister, was one of the first to obtain a degree at Oxford. A bibliophile and scholar (despite her comment in the following story that girls do not make good bibliomaniacs), Dorothy Sayers was also a brilliant historian of the detective story, an authority on Dante, and an important writer on religion.

Dorothy Sayers created the detective story that was closer to the traditional novel, a form that continues into today. Many scholars of literary detection maintain that the world of the twentieth century could be recaptured by students in the world of 2073 by a careful reading of detective fiction.

In discussing her own interest in the detective story, Miss Sayers predicted the form that has developed since she first made her comments, and remarked that if the detective story was to live it must go back to where it began in Wilkie Collins's *The Moonstone,* and once again become a "novel of manners" instead of a pure crossword puzzle. Her character Peter Wimsey had to become "a complete human being, with a past and a future, with a consistent family and social history, with a complicated psychology and even the rudiments of a religious outlook."

Although he appears in many novels, Lord Peter may be best captured in the short story. As Miss Sayers points out, the detective novel itself has the shape of a short story, although it may be expanded to eighty or a hundred thousand words.

"It will be found," she said, "on the whole that the best detective short stories are those which are concerned with a single, not too complicated, twist or trick, not demanding long-drawn-out preparation and explanation.

"Nor," said Miss Sayers, "is literary English always necessary in a detective story [in contrast to the supernatural or horror tale which needs "literary embellishment"], but there must be a central theme strong enough to stand firmly on a basis of clear, grammatical and unpretentious statement."

A wry sense of humor also helps. Miss Sayers had a delightful wit and gave us a refreshing picture of the detective writer:

"Detective authors are nearly all as good as gold because it is part of their job to believe and maintain that Your Sin Will Find You Out. That is why Detective Fiction is, or should be, such a good influence in a degenerate world, and that, no doubt, is why so many bishops, schoolmasters, eminent statesmen and others with reputations to support, read detective stories, to improve their morals and keep themselves out of mischief."

The Learned Adventure of the Dragon's Head

'Uncle Peter!'

'Half a jiff, Gherkins. No, I don't think I'll take the Catullus, Mr Ffolliott. After all, thirteen guineas is a bit steep without either the title or the last folio, what? But you might send me round the Vitruvius and the Satyricon when they come in; I'd like to have a look at them, anyhow. Well, old man, what is it?'

'Do come and look at these pictures, Uncle Peter. I'm sure it's an awfully old book.'

Lord Peter Wimsey sighed as he picked his way out of Mr Ffolliott's dark back shop, strewn with the flotsam and jetsam of many libraries. An unexpected outbreak of measles at Mr Bultridge's excellent preparatory school, coinciding with the absence of the Duke and Duchess of Denver on the Continent, had saddled his lordship with his ten-year-old nephew, Viscount St George, more commonly known as Young Jerry, Jerrykins, or Pickled Gherkins. Lord Peter was not one of those born uncles who delight old nurses by their fascinating 'way with' children. He succeeded, however, in earning tolerance on honourable terms by treating the young with the same scrupulous politeness which he extended to their elders. He therefore prepared to receive Gherkins's discovery with respect, though a child's taste was not to be trusted, and the book might quite well be some horror of woolly mezzotints or an inferior modern reprint adorned with leprous electros. Nothing much better was really to be expected from the 'cheap shelf' exposed to the dust of the street.

'Uncle! there's such a funny man here, with a great long nose and ears and a tail and dogs' heads all over his body. *Monstrum hoc Cracoviae*—that's a monster, isn't it? I should jolly well think it was. What's *Cracoviae*, Uncle Peter?'

'Oh,' said Lord Peter, greatly relieved, 'the Cracow monster?' A portrait of that distressing infant certainly argued a respectable antiquity. 'Let's have a look. Quite right, it's a very old book—Munster's *Cosmographia Universalis*. I'm glad you know good stuff when you see it, Gherkins. What's the *Cosmographia* doing out here, Mr Ffolliott, at five bob?'

'Well, my lord,' said the bookseller, who had followed his customers to the door, 'it's in a very bad state, you see; covers loose and nearly all the double-page maps missing. It came in a few weeks ago—dumped in with a collection we bought from a gentleman in Norfolk—you'll find his name in it—Dr Conyers of Yelsall Manor. Of course, we might keep it and try to make up a complete copy when we get another example. But it's rather out of our line, as you know, classical authors being our speciality. So we just put it out to go for what it would fetch in the *status quo*, as you might say.'

'Oh, look!' broke in Gherkins. 'Here's a picture of a man being chopped up in little bits. What does it say about it?'

'I thought you could read Latin.'

'Well, but it's all full of sort of pothooks. What do they mean?'

'They're just contractions,' said Lord Peter patiently. ' "*Solent quoque hujus insulae cultores*"—It is the custom of the dwellers in this island, when they see their parents stricken in years and of no further use, to take them down into the market-place and sell them to the cannibals, who kill them and eat them for food.

This they do also with younger persons when they fall into any desperate sickness.'

'Ha, ha!' said Mr Ffolliott. 'Rather sharp practice on the poor cannibals. They never got anything but tough old joints or diseased meat, eh?'

'The inhabitants seem to have had thoroughly advanced notions of business,' agreed his lordship.

The viscount was enthralled.

'I *do* like this book,' he said; 'could I buy it out of my pocket-money, please?'

'Another problem for uncles,' thought Lord Peter, rapidly ransacking his recollections of the *Cosmographia* to determine whether any of its illustrations were indelicate; for he knew the duchess to be straitlaced. On consideration, he could only remember one that was dubious, and there was a sporting chance that the duchess might fail to light upon it.

'Well,' he said judicially, 'in your place, Gherkins, I should be inclined to buy it. It's in a bad state, as Mr Ffolliott has honourably told you—otherwise, of course, it would be exceedingly valuable; but, apart from the lost pages, it's a very nice clean copy, and certainly worth five shillings to you, if you think of starting a collection.'

Till that moment, the viscount had obviously been more impressed by the cannibals than by the state of the margins, but the idea of figuring next term at Mr Bultridge's as a collector of rare editions had undeniable charm.

'None of the other fellows collect books,' he said; 'they collect stamps, mostly. I think stamps are rather ordinary, don't you, Uncle Peter? I was rather thinking of giving up stamps. Mr Porter, who takes us for history, has got a lot of books like yours, and he is a splendid man at footer.'

Rightly interpreting this reference to Mr Porter, Lord Peter gave it as his opinion that book-collecting could be a perfectly manly pursuit. Girls, he said, practically never took it up, because it meant so much learning about dates and type-faces and other technicalities which called for a masculine brain.

'Besides,' he added, 'it's a very interesting book in itself, you know. Well worth dipping into.'

'I'll take it, please,' said the viscount, blushing a little at transacting so important and expensive a piece of business; for the duchess did not encourage lavish spending by little boys, and was strict in the matter of allowances.

Mr Ffolliott bowed, and took the *Cosmographia* away to wrap it up.

'Are you all right for cash?' inquired Lord Peter discreetly. 'Or can I be of temporary assistance?'

'No, thank you, uncle; I've got Aunt Mary's half-crown and four shillings of my pocket-money, because, you see, with the measles happening, we didn't have our dormitory spread, and I was saving up for that.'

The business being settled in this gentlemanly manner, and the budding bibliophile taking personal and immediate charge of the stout, square volume, a taxi was chartered which, in due course of traffic delays, brought the *Cosmographia* to 110A Piccadilly.

'And who, Bunter, is Mr Wilberforce Pope?'

'I do not think we know the gentleman, my lord. He is asking to see your lordship for a few minutes on business.'

'He probably wants me to find a lost dog for his maiden aunt. What it is to have acquired a reputation as a sleuth! Show him in. Gherkins, if this good gentleman's business turns out to be private, you'd better retire into the dining-room.'

'Yes, Uncle Peter,' said the viscount dutifully. He was extended on his stomach on the library hearthrug, laboriously picking his way through the more exciting-looking bits of the

Cosmographia, with the aid of Messrs Lewis & Short, whose monumental compilation he had hitherto looked upon as a barbarous invention for the annoyance of upper forms.

Mr Wilberforce Pope turned out to be a rather plump, fair gentleman in the late thirties, with a prematurely bald forehead, horn-rimmed spectacles, and an engaging manner.

'You will excuse my intrusion, won't you?' he began. 'I'm sure you must think me a terrible nuisance. But I wormed your name and address out of Mr Ffolliott. Not his fault, really. You won't blame him, will you? I positively badgered the poor man. Sat down on his doorstep and refused to go, though the boy was putting up the shutters. I'm afraid you will think me very silly when you know what it's all about. But you really mustn't hold poor Mr Ffolliott responsible, now, will you?'

'Not at all,' said his lordship. 'I mean, I'm charmed and all that sort of thing. Something I can do for you about books? You're a collector, perhaps? Will you have a drink or anything?'

'Well, no,' said Mr Pope, with a faint giggle. 'No, not exactly a collector. Thank you very much, just a spot—no, no, literally a spot. Thank you; no'—he glanced round the bookshelves, with their rows of rich old leather bindings—'certainly not a collector. But I happen to be er, interested—sentimentally interested—in a purchase you made yesterday. Really, such a very small matter. You will think it foolish. But I am told you are the present owner of a copy of Munster's *Cosmographia,* which used to belong to my uncle, Dr Conyers.'

Gherkins looked up suddenly, seeing that the conversation had a personal interest for him.

'Well, that's not quite correct,' said Wimsey. 'I was there at the time, but the actual purchaser is my nephew. Gerald, Mr Pope is interested in your *Cosmographia.* My nephew, Lord St George.'

'How do you do, young man,' said Mr Pope affably. 'I see

that the collecting spirit runs in the family. A great Latin scholar, too, I expect, eh? Ready to decline *jusjurandum* with the best of us? Ha, ha! And what are you going to do when you grow up? Be Lord Chancellor, eh? Now, I bet you think you'd rather be an engine-driver, what, what?'

'No, thank you,' said the viscount, with aloofness.

'What, not an engine-driver? Well, now, I want you to be a real business man this time. Put through a book deal, you know. Your uncle will see I offer you a fair price, what? Ha, ha! Now, you see, that picture-book of yours has a great value for me that it wouldn't have for anybody else. When *I* was a little boy of your age it was one of my very greatest joys. I used to have it to look at on Sundays. Ah, dear! the happy hours I used to spend with those quaint old engravings, and the funny old maps with the ships and salamanders and *"Hic dracones"*—you know what *that* means, I dare say. What does it mean?'

'Here are dragons,' said the viscount, unwillingly but still politely.

'Quite right. I *knew* you were a scholar.'

'It's a very attractive book,' said Lord Peter. 'My nephew was quite entranced by the famous Cracow monster.'

'Ah yes—a glorious monster, isn't it?' agreed Mr Pope, with enthusiasm. 'Many's the time I've fancied myself as Sir Lancelot or somebody on a white war horse, charging that monster, lance in rest, with the captive princess cheering me on. Ah! childhood! You're living the happiest days of your life, young man. You won't believe me, but you are.'

'Now what is it exactly you want my nephew to do?' inquired Lord Peter a little sharply.

'Quite right, quite right. Well now, you know, my uncle, Dr Conyers, sold his library a few months ago. I was abroad at the time, and it was only yesterday, when I went down to Yel-

The Learned Adventure of the Dragon's Head | 77

sall on a visit, that I learnt the dear old book had gone with the rest. I can't tell you how distressed I was. I know it's not valuable—a great many pages missing and all that—but I can't bear to think of its being gone. So, purely from sentimental reasons, as I said, I hurried off to Ffolliott's to see if I could get it back. I was quite upset to find I was too late, and gave poor Mr Ffolliott no peace till he told me the name of the purchaser. Now, you see, Lord St George, I'm here to make you an offer for the book. Come, now, double what you gave for it. That's a good offer, isn't it, Lord Peter? Ha, ha! And you will be doing me a very great kindness as well.'

Viscount St George looked rather distressed, and turned appealingly to his uncle.

'Well, Gerald,' said Lord Peter, 'it's your affair, you know. What do you say?'

The viscount stood first on one leg and then on the other. The career of a book collector evidently had its problems, like other careers.

'If you please, Uncle Peter,' he said, with embarrassment, 'may I whisper?'

'It's not usually considered the thing to whisper, Gherkins, but you could ask Mr Pope for time to consider his offer. Or you could say you would prefer to consult me first. That would be quite in order.'

'Then, if you don't mind, Mr Pope, I should like to consult my uncle first.'

'Certainly, certainly; ha, ha!' said Mr Pope. 'Very prudent to consult a collector of greater experience, what? Ah! the younger generation, eh, Lord Peter? Regular little business men already.'

'Excuse us, then, for one moment,' said Lord Peter, and drew his nephew into the dining-room.

'I say, Uncle Peter,' said the collector breathlessly, when the door was shut, '*need* I 'give him my book? I don't think he's a very nice man. I *hate* people who ask you to decline nouns for them.'

'Certainly you needn't, Gherkins, if you don't want to. The book is yours, and you've a right to it.'

'What would *you* do, uncle?'

Before replying, Lord Peter, in the most surprising manner, tiptoed gently to the door which communicated with the library and flung it suddenly open, in time to catch Mr Pope kneeling on the hearthrug intently turning over the pages of the coveted volume, which lay as the owner had left it. He started to his feet in a flurried manner as the door opened.

'Do help yourself, Mr Pope, won't you?' cried Lord Peter hospitably, and closed the door again.

'What is it, Uncle Peter?'

'If you want my advice, Gherkins, I should be rather careful how you had any dealings with Mr Pope. I don't think he's telling the truth. He called those wood-cuts engravings—though, of course, that may be just his ignorance. But I can't believe that he spent all his childhood's Sunday afternoons studying those maps and picking out the dragons in them, because, as you may have noticed for yourself, old Munster put very few dragons into his maps. They're mostly just plain maps—a bit queer to our ideas of geography, but perfectly straightforward. That was why I brought in the Cracow monster, and, you see, he thought it was some sort of dragon.'

'Oh, I say, uncle! So you said that on purpose!'

'If Mr Pope wants the *Cosmographia*, it's for some reason he doesn't want to tell us about. And, that being so, I wouldn't be in too big a hurry to sell, if the book were mine. See?'

'Do you mean there's something frightfully valuable about the book, which we don't know?'

'Possibly.'

'How exciting! It's just like a story in the *Boys' Friend Library*. What am I to say to him, uncle?'

'Well, in your place I wouldn't be dramatic or anything. I'd just say you've considered the matter, and you've taken a fancy to the book and have decided not to sell. You thank him for his offer, of course.'

'Yes—er, won't you say it for me, uncle?'

'I think it would look better if you did it yourself.'

'Yes, perhaps it would. Will he be very cross?'

'Possibly,' said Lord Peter, 'but if he is, he won't let on. Ready?'

The consulting committee accordingly returned to the library. Mr Pope had prudently retired from the hearthrug and was examining a distant bookcase.

'Thank you very much for your offer, Mr Pope,' said the viscount, striding stoutly up to him, 'but I have considered it, and I have taken a—a—a fancy for the book and decided not to sell.'

'Sorry and all that,' put in Lord Peter, 'but my nephew's adamant about it. No, it isn't the price; he wants the book. Wish I could oblige you, but it isn't in my hands. Won't you take something else before you go? Really? Ring the bell, Gherkins. My man will see you to the lift. *Good* evening.'

When the visitor had gone, Lord Peter returned and thoughtfully picked up the book.

'We were awful idiots to leave him with it, Gherkins, even for a moment. Luckily, there's no harm done.'

'You don't think he found out anything while we were away, do you, uncle?' gasped Gherkins, open-eyed.

'I'm sure he didn't.'

'Why?'

'He offered me fifty pounds for it on the way to the door. Gave the game away. H'm! Bunter.'

'My lord?'

'Put this book in the safe and bring me back the keys. And you'd better set all the burglar alarms when you lock up.'

'Oo—er!' said Viscount St George.

On the third morning after the visit of Mr Wilberforce Pope, the viscount was seated at a very late breakfast in his uncle's flat, after the most glorious and soul-satisfying night that ever boy experienced. He was almost too excited to eat the kidneys and bacon placed before him by Bunter, whose usual impeccable manner was not in the least impaired by a rapidly swelling and blackening eye.

It was about two in the morning that Gherkins—who had not slept very well, owing to too lavish and grown-up a dinner and theatre the evening before—became aware of a stealthy sound somewhere in the direction of the fire-escape. He had got out of bed and crept very softly into Lord Peter's room and woken him up. He had said: 'Uncle Peter, I'm sure there's burglars on the fire-escape.' And Uncle Peter, instead of saying, 'Nonsense, Gherkins, hurry up and get back to bed,' had sat up and listened and said: 'By Jove, Gherkins, I believe you're right.' And had sent Gherkins to call Bunter. And on his return, Gherkins, who had always regarded his uncle as a very top-hatted sort of person, actually saw him take from his handkerchief-drawer an undeniable automatic pistol.

It was at this point that Lord Peter was apotheosed from the state of Quite Decent Uncle to that of Glorified Uncle. He said:

'Look here, Gherkins, we don't know how many of these blighters there'll be, so you must be jolly smart and do anything I say sharp, on the word of command—even if I have to say "Scoot". Promise?'

Gherkins promised, with his heart thumping, and they sat waiting in the dark, till suddenly a little electric bell rang sharply just over the head of Lord Peter's bed and a green light shone out.

'The library window,' said his lordship, promptly silencing the bell by turning a switch. 'If they heard, they may think better of it. We'll give them a few minutes.'

They gave them five minutes, and then crept very quietly down the passage.

'Go round by the dining-room, Bunter,' said his lordship; 'they may bolt that way.'

With infinite precaution, he unlocked and opened the library door, and Gherkins noticed how silently the locks moved.

A circle of light from an electric torch was moving slowly along the bookshelves. The burglars had obviously heard nothing of the counter-attack. Indeed, they seemed to have troubles enough of their own to keep their attention occupied. As his eyes grew accustomed to the dim light, Gherkins made out that one man was standing holding the torch, while the other took down and examined the books. It was fascinating to watch his apparently disembodied hands move along the shelves in the torch-light.

The men muttered discontentedly. Obviously the job was proving a harder one than they had bargained for. The habit of ancient authors of abbreviating the titles on the backs of their volumes, or leaving them completely untitled, made things extremely awkward. From time to time the man with the torch extended his hand into the light. It held a piece of paper, which they anxiously compared with the title-page of a book. Then the volume was replaced and the tedious search went on.

Suddenly some slight noise—Gherkins was sure *he* did not make it; it may have been Bunter in the dining-room—seemed to catch the ear of the kneeling man.

'Wot's that?' he gasped, and his startled face swung round into view.

'Hands up!' said Lord Peter, and switched the light on.

The second man made one leap for the dining-room door, where a smash and an oath proclaimed that he had encountered Bunter. The kneeling man shot his hands up like a marionette.

'Gherkins,' said Lord Peter, 'do you think you can go across to that gentleman by the bookcase and relieve him of the article which is so inelegantly distending the right-hand pocket of his coat? Wait a minute. Don't on any account get between him and my pistol, and mind you take the thing out *very* carefully. There's no hurry. That's splendid. Just point it at the floor while you bring it across, would you? Thanks. Bunter has managed for himself, I see. Now run into my bedroom, and in the bottom of my wardrobe you will find a bundle of stout cord. Oh! I beg your pardon; yes, put your hands down by all means. It must be very tiring exercise.'

The arms of the intruders being secured behind their backs with a neatness which Gherkins felt to be worthy of the best traditions of Sexton Blake, Lord Peter motioned his captives to sit down and despatched Bunter for whisky-and-soda.

'Before we send for the police,' said Lord Peter, 'you would do me a great personal favour by telling me what you were looking for, and who sent you. Ah! thanks, Bunter. As our guests are not at liberty to use their hands, perhaps you would be kind enough to assist them to a drink. Now then, say when.'

'Well, you're a gentleman, guv'nor,' said the First Burglar, wiping his mouth politely on his shoulder, the back of his hand not being available. 'If we'd a known wot a job this wos goin' ter be, blow me if we'd a touched it. The bloke said, ses 'e, "It's takin' candy from a baby," 'e ses. "The gentleman's a reg'lar softie," 'e ses, "one o' these 'ere sersiety toffs wiv a maggot fer old books," that's wot 'e ses, "an' ef yer can find this 'ere old book fer me," 'e ses, "there's a pony fer yer." Well! Sech a job! 'E didn't mention as 'ow there'd be five 'undred fousand bleedin' ole books all as alike as a regiment o' bleedin' dragoons. Nor as 'ow yer kept a nice little machine-gun like that 'andy by the bedside, *nor* yet as 'ow yer was so bleedin' good at tyin' knots in a bit o' string. No—'e didn't think ter mention them things.'

'Deuced unsporting of him,' said his lordship. 'Do you happen to know the gentleman's name?'

'No—that was another o' them things wot 'e didn't mention. 'E's a stout, fair party, wiv 'orn rims to 'is goggles and a bald 'ead. One o' these 'ere philanthropists, I reckon. A friend o' mine, wot got inter trouble onct, got work froo 'im, and the gentleman comes round and ses to 'im, 'e ses, "Could yer find me a couple o' lads ter do a little job?" 'e ses, an' my friend finkin' no 'arm, you see, guv'nor, but wot it might be a bit of a joke like, 'e gets 'old of my pal an' me, an' we meets the gentleman in a pub dahn Whitechapel way. W'ich we was ter meet 'im there again Friday night, us 'avin' allowed that time fer ter git 'old of the book.'

'The book being, if I may hazard a guess, the *Cosmographia Universalis*?'

'Sumfink like that, guv'nor. I got its jaw-breakin' name wrote down on a bit o' paper, wot my pal 'ad in 'is 'and. Wot did yer do wiv that 'ere bit o' paper, Bill?'

'Well, look here,' said Lord Peter, 'I'm afraid I must send for the police, but I think it likely, if you give us your assistance to get hold of your gentleman, whose name I strangely suspect to be Wilberforce Pope, that you will get off pretty easily. Telephone the police, Bunter, and then go and put something on that eye of yours. Gherkins, we'll give these gentlemen another drink, and then I think perhaps you'd better hop back to bed; the fun's over. No? Well, put a good thick coat on, there's a good fellow, because what your mother will say to me if you catch a cold I don't like to think.'

So the police had come and taken the burglars away, and now Detective-Inspector Parker, of Scotland Yard, a great personal friend of Lord Peter's, sat toying with a cup of coffee and listening to the story.

'But what's the matter with the jolly old book, anyhow, to make it so popular?' he demanded.

'I don't know,' replied Wimsey; 'but after Mr Pope's little visit the other day I got kind of intrigued about it and had a look through it. I've got a hunch it may turn out rather valuable, after all. Unsuspected beauties and all that sort of thing. If only Mr Pope had been a trifle more accurate in his facts, he might have got away with something to which I feel pretty sure he isn't entitled. Anyway, when I'd seen—what I saw, I wrote off to Dr Conyers of Yelsall Manor, the late owner—'

'Conyers, the cancer man?'

'Yes. He's done some pretty important research in his time, I fancy. Getting on now, though; about seventy-eight, I fancy. I hope he's more honest than his nephew, with one foot in the grave like that. Anyway, I wrote (with Gherkins's permission, naturally) to say we had the book and had been specially interested by something we found there, and would he be so obliging as to tell us something of its history. I also—'

'But what did you find in it?'

'I don't think we'll tell him yet, Gherkins, shall we? I like to keep policemen guessing. As I was saying, when you so rudely interrupted me, I also asked him whether he knew anything about his good nephew's offer to buy it back. His answer has just arrived. He says he knows of nothing specially interesting about the book. It has been in the library untold years, and the tearing out of the maps must have been done a long time ago by some family vandal. He can't think why his nephew should be so keen on it, as he certainly never pored over it as a boy. In fact, the old man declares the engaging Wilberforce has never even set foot in Yelsall Manor to his knowledge. So much for the fire-breathing monsters and the pleasant Sunday afternoons.'

'Naughty Wilberforce!'

'M'm. Yes. So, after last night's little dust-up, I wired the old boy we were tooling down to Yelsall to have a heart-to-heart talk with him about his picture-book and his nephew.'

'Are you taking the book down with you?' asked Parker. 'I can give you a police escort for it if you like.'

'That's not a bad idea,' said Wimsey. 'We don't know where the insinuating Mr Pope may be hanging out, and I wouldn't put it past him to make another attempt.'

'Better be on the safe side,' said Parker. 'I can't come myself, but I'll send down a couple of men with you.'

'Good egg,' said Lord Peter. 'Call up your myrmidons. We'll get a car round at once. You're coming, Gherkins, I suppose? God knows what your mother would say. 'Don't ever be an uncle, Charles; it's frightfully difficult to be fair to all parties.'

Yelsall Manor was one of those large, decaying country mansions which speak eloquently of times more spacious than our own. The original late Tudor construction had been masked by the addition of a wide frontage in the Italian manner, with a kind of classical portico surmounted by a pediment and approached by a semi-circular flight of steps. The grounds had originally been laid out in that formal manner in which grove nods to grove and each half duly reflects the other. A late owner, however, had burst out into the more eccentric sort of landscape gardening which is associated with the name of Capability Brown. A Chinese pagoda, somewhat resembling Sir William Chambers's erection in Kew Gardens, but smaller, rose out of a grove of laurustinus towards the eastern extremity of the house, while at the rear appeared a large artificial lake, dotted with numerous islands, on which odd little temples, grottos, tea-houses, and bridges peeped out from among clumps of shrubs, once ornamental, but now sadly overgrown. A boat-house, with wide eaves like the designs on a willow-pattern plate, stood at one corner, its landing-stage fallen into decay and wreathed with melancholy weeds.

'My disreputable old ancestor, Cuthbert Conyers, settled down here when he retired from the sea in 1732,' said Dr Conyers, smiling faintly. 'His elder brother died childless, so the black sheep returned to the fold with the determination to become respectable and found a family. I fear he did not succeed altogether. There were very queer tales as to where his money came from. He is said to have been a pirate, and to have sailed with the notorious Captain Blackbeard. In the village, to this day, he is remembered and spoken of as Cut-throat Conyers. It used to make the old man very angry, and there is an unpleasant story of his slicing the ears off a groom who had been heard to call him "Old Cut-throat". He was not an uncultivated person, though. It was he who did the landscape-gardening round at the back, and he built the pagoda for his telescope. He was reputed to study the Black Art, and there were certainly a number of astrological works in the library with his name on the fly-leaf, but probably the telescope was only a remembrance of his seafaring days.

'Anyhow, towards the end of his life he became more and more odd and morose. He quarrelled with his family, and turned his younger son out of doors with his wife and children. An unpleasant old fellow.

'On his deathbed he was attended by the parson—a good, earnest, God-fearing sort of man, who must have put up with a deal of insult in carrying out what he firmly believed to be the sacred duty of reconciling the old man to this shamefully treated son. Eventually, "Old Cut-throat" relented so far as to make a will, leaving to the younger son "My treasure which I have buried in Munster". The parson represented to him that it was useless to bequeath a treasure unless he also bequeathed the information where to find it, but the horrid old pirate only chuckled spitefully, and said that, as he had been at the pains to collect the treasure, his son might well be at the pains of looking for it. Further than that he would not go, and so he died, and I dare say went to a very bad place.

'Since then the family has died out, and I am the sole representative of the Conyers, and heir to the treasure, whatever and wherever it is, for it was never discovered. I do not suppose it was very honestly come by, but, since it would be useless now to try and find the original owners, I imagine I have a better right to it than anybody living.

'You may think it very unseemly, Lord Peter, that an old, lonely man like myself should be greedy for a hoard of pirate's gold. But my whole life has been devoted to studying the disease of cancer, and I believe myself to be very close to a solution of one part at least of the terrible problem. Research costs money, and my limited means are very nearly exhausted. The property is mortgaged up to the hilt, and I do most urgently desire to complete my experiments before I die, and to leave a sufficient sum to found a clinic where the work can be carried on.

'During the last year I have made very great efforts to solve the mystery of "Old Cut-throat's" treasure. I have been able to leave much of my experimental work in the most capable hands of my assistant, Dr Forbes, while I pursued my researches with the very slender clue I had to go upon. It was the more expensive and difficult that Cuthbert had left no indication in his will whether Münster in Germany or Munster in Ireland was the hiding-place of the treasure. My journeys and my search in both places cost money and brought me no further on my quest. I returned, disheartened, in August, and found myself obliged to sell my library, in order to defray my expenses and obtain a little money with which to struggle on with my sadly delayed experiments.'

'Ah!' said Lord Peter. 'I begin to see light.'

The old physician looked at him inquiringly. They had finished tea, and were seated around the great fireplace in the study. Lord Peter's interested questions about the beautiful, dilapidated old house and estate had led the conversation naturally to Dr Conyers's family, shelving for the time the problem of the *Cosmographia*, which lay on a table beside them.

'Everything you say fits into the puzzle,' went on Wimsey, 'and I think there's not the smallest doubt what Mr Wilberforce Pope was after, though how he knew that you had the *Cosmographia* here I couldn't say.'

'When I disposed of the library, I sent him a catalogue,' said Dr Conyers. 'As a relative, I thought he ought to have the right to buy anything he fancied. I can't think why he didn't secure the book then, instead of behaving in this most shocking fashion.'

Lord Peter hooted with laughter.

'Why, because he never tumbled to it till afterwards,' he said. 'And oh, dear, how wild he must have been! I forgive him everything. Although,' he added, 'I don't want to raise your hopes too high, sir, for, even when we've solved old Cuthbert's riddle, I don't know that we're very much nearer to the treasure.'

'To the *treasure*?'

'Well, now, sir. I want you first to look at this page, where there's a name scrawled in the margin. Our ancestors had an untidy way of signing their possessions higgledy-piggledy in margins instead of in a decent, Christian way in the fly-leaf. This is a handwriting of somewhere about Charles I's reign: "Jac: Coniers". I take it that goes to prove that the book was in the possession of your family at any rate as early as the first half of the seventeenth century, and has remained there ever since. Right, now we turn to page 1099, where we find a description of the discoveries of Christopher Columbus. It's headed, you see, by a kind of map, with some of Mr Pope's monsters swim-

Liber V. 1099
DE NOVIS INSVLIS,
quomodo, quando, & per quem
illæ inuentæ sint.

Hriſtophorus Columbus natione Genuenſis, cùm diu in aula regis Hiſpan′
rum deuerſatus fuiſſet, animum induxit, ut hactenus inacceſſas orbis partes p
aoraret. Petut præterea à rege ut ubi ſuo non deeſſet futurū ſibi & roti Hiſ₋

ming about in it, and apparently representing the Canaries, or, as they used to be called, the Fortunate Isles. It doesn't look much more accurate than old maps usually are, but I take it the big island on the right is meant for Lanzarote, and the two nearest to it may be Teneriffe and Gran Canaria.'

'But what's that writing in the middle?'

'That's just the point. The writing is later than "Jac: Coniers's" signature; I should put it about 1700—but, of course, it may have been written a good deal later still. I mean, a man who was elderly in 1730 would still use the style of writing he adopted as a young man, especially if, like your ancestor the pirate, he had spent the early part of his life in outdoor pursuits and hadn't done much writing.'

'Do you mean to say, Uncle Peter,' broke in the viscount excitedly, 'that that's "Old Cut-throat's" writing?'

'I'd be ready to lay a sporting bet it is. Look here, sir, you've been scouring round Münster in Germany and Munster in Ireland—but how about good old Sebastian Munster here in the library at home?'

'God bless my soul! Is it possible?'

'It's pretty nearly certain, sir. Here's what he says, written, you see, round the head of that sort of sea-dragon:

> Hic in capite draconis ardet perpetuo Sol.
> Here the sun shines perpetually upon the Dragon's Head.

Rather doggy Latin—sea-dog Latin, you might say, in fact.'

'I'm afraid,' said Dr Conyers, 'I must be very stupid, but I can't see where that leads us.'

'No: "Old Cut-throat" was rather clever. No doubt he thought that, if anybody read it, they'd think it was just an allusion to where it says, further down, that "the islands were called *Fortunatae* because of the wonderful temperature of the air and the clemency of the skies." But the cunning old astrologer up in his pagoda had a meaning of his own. Here's a little book published in 1678—Middleton's *Practical Astrology*—just the sort of popular handbook an amateur like "Old Cut-throat" would use. Here you are: "If in your figure you find Jupiter or Venus or *Dragon's head*, you may be confident there is Treasure in the place supposed. . . . If you find *Sol* to be the significator of the hidden Treasure, you may conclude there is Gold, or some jewels." You know, sir, I think we may conclude it.'

'Dear me!' said Dr Conyers. 'I believe, indeed, you must be right. And I am ashamed to think that if anybody had suggested to me that it could ever be profitable to me to learn the terms of astrology, I should have replied in my vanity that my time was too valuable to waste on such foolishness. I am deeply indebted to you.'

'Yes,' said Gherkins, 'but where *is* the treasure, uncle?'

'That's just it,' said Lord Peter. 'The map is very vague; there is no latitude or longitude given; and the directions, such as they are, seem not even to refer to any spot on the islands, but to some place in the middle of the sea. Besides, it is nearly two hundred years since the treasure was hidden, and it may already have been found by somebody or other.'

Dr Conyers stood up.

'I am an old man,' he said, 'but I still have some strength. If I can by any means get together the money for an expedition, I will not rest till I have made every possible effort to find the treasure and to endow my clinic.'

'Then, sir, I hope you'll let me give a hand to the good work,' said Lord Peter.

Dr Conyers had invited his guests to stay the night, and, after the excited viscount had been packed off to bed, Wimsey and the old man sat late, consulting maps and diligently reading Munster's chapter 'De Novis Insulis', in the hope of discovering some further clue. At length, however, they separated, and Lord Peter went upstairs, the book under his arm. He was restless, however, and, instead of going to bed, sat for a long time at his window, which looked out upon the lake. The moon, a few days past the full, was riding high among small, windy clouds, and picked out the sharp eaves of the Chinese tea-houses and the straggling tops of the unpruned shrubs. 'Old Cut-throat' and his landscape gardening! Wimsey could have fancied that the old pirate was sitting now beside his telescope in the preposterous pagoda, chuckling over his riddling testament and counting the craters of the moon. 'If *Luna*, there is silver,' The waters of the lake was silver enough; there was a great smooth path across it, broken by the sinister wedge of the boat-house, the black shadows of the islands, and, almost in the middle of the lake, a decayed fountain, a writhing Celestial dragon-shape, spiny-backed and ridiculous.

Wimsey rubbed his eyes. There was something strangely familiar about the lake; from moment to moment it assumed the queer unreality of a place which one recognizes without having ever known it. It was like one's first sight of the Leaning Tower of Pisa—too like its picture to be quite believable. Surely, thought Wimsey, he knew that elongated island on the right, shaped rather like a winged monster, with its two little clumps of buildings. And the island to the left of it, like the British Isles, but warped out of shape. And the third island, between the others, and nearer. The three formed a triangle, with the Chinese fountain in the centre, the moon shining steadily upon its dragon head. *Hic in capite draconis ardet perpetuo—*

Lord Peter sprang up with a loud exclamation, and flung open the door into the dressing-room. A small figure wrapped in an eiderdown hurriedly uncoiled itself from the window-seat.

'I'm sorry, Uncle Peter,' said Gherkins, 'I was so *dreadfully* wide awake, it wasn't any good staying in bed.'

'Come here,' said Lord Peter, 'and tell me if I'm mad or dreaming. Look out of the window and compare it with the map—"Old Cut-throat's" "New Islands". He made 'em, Gherkins; he put 'em here. Aren't they laid out just like the Canaries? Those three islands in a triangle, and the fourth down here in the corner? And the boat-house where the big ship is in the picture? And the dragon fountain where the dragon's head is? Well, my son, that's where your hidden treasure's gone to. Get your things on, Gherkins, and damn the time when all good little boys should be in bed! We're going for a row on the lake, if there's a tub in that boat-house that'll float.'

'Oh, Uncle Peter! This is a *real* adventure!'

'All right,' said Wimsey. 'Fifteen men on the dead man's chest, and all that! Yo-ho-ho, and a bottle of Johnny Walker! Pirate expedition fitted out in dead of night to seek hidden treasure and explore the Fortunate Isles! Come on, crew!'

Lord Peter hitched the leaky dinghy to the dragon's knobbly tail and climbed out carefully, for the base of the fountain was green and weedy.

'I'm afraid it's your job to sit there and bail, Gherkins,' he said. 'All the best captains bag the really interesting jobs for themselves. We'd better start with the head. If the old blighter said head, he probably meant it.' He passed an arm affectionately round the creature's neck for support, while he methodically pressed and pulled the various knobs and bumps of its anatomy. 'It seems beastly solid, but I'm sure there's a spring somewhere. You won't forget to bail, will you? I'd simply hate to turn round and find the boat gone. Pirate chief marooned on island and all that. Well, it isn't its back hair, anyhow. We'll try its eyes. I say, Gherkins, I'm sure I felt something move, only it's frightfully stiff. We might have thought to bring some oil. Never mind; it's dogged as does it. It's coming. It's coming. Booh! Pah!'

A fierce effort thrust the rusted knob inwards, releasing a huge spout of water into his face from the dragon's gaping throat. The fountain, dry for many years, soared rejoicingly heavenwards, drenching the treasure-hunters, and making rainbows in the moonlight.

'I suppose this is "Old Cut-throat's" idea of humour,' grumbled Wimsey, retreating cautiously round the dragon's neck. 'And now I can't turn it off again. Well, dash it all, let's try the other eye.'

He pressed for a few moments in vain. Then, with a grinding clang, the bronze wings of the monster clapped down to its sides, revealing a deep square hole, and the fountain ceased to play.

'Gherkins!' said Lord Peter, 'we've done it. (But don't neglect bailing on that account!) There's a box here. And it's beastly heavy. No; all right, I can manage. Gimme the boat-hook. Now I do hope the old sinner really did have a treasure. What a bore if it's only one of his little jokes. Never mind—hold the boat steady. There. Always remember, Gherkins, that you can make quite an effective crane with a boat-hook and a stout pair of braces. Got it? That's right. Now for home and beauty. . . . Hullo! what's all that?'

As he paddled the boat round, it was evident that something was happening down by the boat-house. Lights were moving about, and a sound of voices came across the lake.

'They think we're burglars, Gherkins. Always misunderstood. Give way, my hearties—

> 'A-roving, a-roving, since roving's been my ru-i-in,
> I'll go no more a-roving with you, fair maid.'

'Is that you, my lord?' said a man's voice as they drew in to the boat-house.

'Why, it's our faithful sleuths!' cried his lordship. 'What's the excitement?'

'We found this fellow sneaking round the boat-house,' said the man from Scotland Yard. 'He says he's the old gentleman's nephew. Do you know him, my lord?'

'I rather fancy I do,' said Wimsey. 'Mr Pope, I think. Good evening. Were you looking for anything? Not a treasure, by any chance? Because we've just found one. Oh! don't say that. *Maxima reverentia*, you know. Lord St George is of tender years. And, by the way, thank you so much for sending your delight-

The Learned Adventure of the Dragon's Head | 95

ful friends to call on me last night. Oh, yes, Thompson, I'll charge him all right. You there, doctor? Splendid. Now, if anybody's got a spanner or anything handy, we'll have a look at Great-grandpapa Cuthbert. And if he turns out to be old iron, Mr Pope, you'll have had an uncommonly good joke for your money.'

An iron bar was produced from the boat-house and thrust under the clasp of the chest. It creaked and burst. Dr Conyers knelt down tremulously and threw open the lid.

There was a little pause.

'The drinks are on you, Mr Pope,' said Lord Peter. 'I think, doctor, it ought to be a jolly good hospital when it's finished.'

※ | Margery Allingham

In the golden years of the detective story, the superman investigator ruled supreme. Who can ever forget Sherlock Holmes, in ulster and deerstalker hat, with his beaked face, that powerful nose scenting out telltale cigar ashes, those wiry hands playing his irascible fiddle, or his laconic conversation, "Elementary, my dear Watson." Holmes was such a fully realized character that he lives in the mind far longer than the author who created him.

The superman or eccentric detective could not last forever. Eventually his place was to be taken by Mr. Average Man—not so average that his identity would not carry him through many books, but certainly more realistic. Such a detective is Margery Allingham's famous Albert Campion. Of course Albert Campion is not so average. In typical British fashion he is introduced as being extremely well bred with perhaps even close connections to royalty. As the author herself said, "The general impression one received from him was that he was well-bred and a trifle absent-minded."

But well-bred or not, unlike Sherlock Holmes or Agatha Christie's Hercule Poirot, he was not memorable for his appearance; one remembers little except he was fair-haired and wore glasses.

Margery Allingham's gift to the detective story was a gentle touch of irony. She had a unique ability to combine "detectionism" with penetrating comment on the social scene. She said of herself, "I am a domesticated person with democratic principles and very few unorthodox convictions. I have no particular ax to grind and I belong to no rigid school of thought, but I am content to hold with the poet that the proper study of mankind is man."

Miss Allingham began her remarkable writing career at the age of seven and had her first novel published at the age of sixteen. She grew up in a small village in Britain, and as an adult lived in rural Essex. Miss Allingham was deeply involved in village affairs as well as being devoted to her horses, dogs, and garden—and, of course, to the reading she loved. She cited Shakespeare, Sterne, and the elder Dumas as "the most influential writers" in her life.

Family Affair

The newspapers were calling the McGill house in Chestnut Grove "the villa Mary Celeste" before Chief-inspector Charles Luke noticed the similarity between the two mysteries and that so shook him that he telephoned Albert Campion and asked him to come over.

They met in the Sun, a discreet pub in suburban High Street, and stood talking in the small bar-parlor which was deserted at that time of day.

"The two stories *are* alike," Luke said, picking up his drink. He was at the height of his career then, a dark, muscular man, high-cheek-boned and packed with energy; and as usual he was talking nineteen to the dozen forcing home his points with characteristic gestures of his long hands. "I read the rehash of the *Mary Celeste* mystery in the *Courier* this morning and it took me to the fair. Except that she was a ship and 29 Chestnut Grove is a semi-detached suburban house, the two desertion stories are virtually the same—even to the half-eaten breakfast left on the table in each case. It's uncanny, Campion."

The quiet, fair man in the hornrimmed glasses stood listening affably, as was his habit. And as usual, he looked vague and probably ineffectual; in the shadier corners of Europe it was said that no one ever took him seriously until just about two hours too late. At the moment he appeared faintly amused. The thumping force of Luke's enthusiasms always tickled him.

"You think you know what has happened to the McGill couple, then?" he ventured.

"The hell I do!" The policeman opened his small black eyes to their widest. "I tell you it's the same tale as the classic mystery of the *Mary Celeste*. They've gone like a stain under a bleach. One minute they were having breakfast together like every other married couple for miles around and the next they were gone, sunk without trace."

Mr. Campion hesitated. He looked a trifle embarrassed. "As I recall the story of the *Mary Celeste* it had the simple charm of the utterly incredible," he said at last. "Let's see: she was a brig brought into Gib by a prize crew of innocent sailormen who had a wonderful tale to tell. According to them, she was sighted in mid-ocean with all her sails set, her decks clean, her lockers tidy, but not a soul on board. The details were fascinating. There were three cups of tea on the captain's table and they were still warm to the touch. There was a trunk of female clothes, small enough to be a child's, in his cabin. There was a cat asleep in the galley and a chicken ready for stewing in a pot on the stove." Campion sighed gently. "Quite beautiful," he said, "but witnesses also swore that with no one at the wheel she was still dead on course and that seemed a little too much for the court of inquiry. After kicking it about as long as they could, they finally made the absolute minimum award."

Luke glanced at him sharply.

"That wasn't the *Courier*'s angle last night," he said. "They called it the 'world's favorite unsolved mystery.' "

"So it is!" Mr. Campion was laughing. "Because nobody wants a prosaic explanation of fraud and greed. The mystery of the *Mary Celeste* is a prime example of the story which really is a bit *too* good to spoil, don't you think?"

"I don't know. It's not an idea which occurred to me." Luke sounded slightly irritated. "I was merely quoting the main outlines of the two tales—1872 and the *Mary Celeste* is a bit before my time. On the other hand, 29 Chestnut Grove is definitely my business and you can take it from me no witness is being allowed to use his imagination in this inquiry. Just give your mind to the details, Campion."

Luke set his tumbler down on the bar and began ticking off each item on his fingers.

"Consider the couple," he said. "They sound normal enough. Peter McGill was twenty-eight and his wife Maureen a year younger. They'd been married three years and got on well together. For the first two years they had to board with his mother while they were waiting for a house. That didn't work out too well, so they rented a couple of rooms from Maureen's married sister. That lasted for six months and then they got the offer of this house in Chestnut Grove."

"Any money troubles?" Mr. Campion asked.

"No." The Chief clearly thought the fact remarkable. "Peter seems to be the one lad in the family who had nothing to grumble about. His firm—they're locksmiths in Aldgate, he's in the office—are very pleased with him. His reputation is that he keeps within his income and he's recently had a raise in salary. I saw the senior partner this morning and he's genuinely worried, poor old boy. He liked the young man and had nothing but praise for him."

"What about Mrs. McGill?"

"She's another good type. Steady, reliable, kept on at her job as a typist until a few months ago when her husband decided she should retire to enjoy the new house and raise a family. She certainly did her housework. The place is still like a new pin and they've been gone six weeks."

For the first time Mr. Campion's eyes darkened with interest. "Forgive me," he said, "but the police seem to have come into this disappearance very quickly. What are you looking for, Charles? A body? Or bodies?"

Luke shrugged. "Not officially," he said, "but one doesn't have to have a nasty mind to wonder. We came in to the investigation quickly because the alarm was given quickly. The circumstances were extraordinary and the family got the wind up. That's the explanation of that." He paused and stood for a moment hesitating. "Come along and have a look," he said, and his restless personality was a live thing in the confined space. "We'll come back and have another drink after you've seen the setup—I've got something really recherché here. I want you in on it."

Mr. Campion followed him out into the network of trim little streets lined with bandbox villas, each set in a nest of flower garden.

"It's just down the end here and along to the right," Luke said, nodding toward the end of the avenue. "I'll give you the rest of it as we go. On the twelfth of June, Bertram Heskith, a somewhat overbright specimen who is the husband of Maureen's elder sister—the one they lodged with, two doors down the road before Number 29 became available—dropped round to see them as he usually did just before eight in the morning. He came in at the back door which was standing open and found a half-eaten breakfast for two on the table in the smart new kitchen. No one was about, so he pulled up a chair and sat down to wait."

Luke's long hands were busy as he talked and Mr. Campion could almost see the bright little room with the built-in furniture and the pot of flowers on the window ledge.

"Bertram is a toy salesman and one of a large family," Luke went on. "He's out of a job at the moment but is not despondent. He's a talkative man, a fraction too big for his clothes now, and he likes his nip—but he's sharp enough. He'd have noticed at once if there had been anything at all unusual to see. As it was, he poured himself a cup of tea out of the pot under the cosy and sat there waiting, reading the newspaper which he found lying open on the floor by Peter McGill's chair. Finally it occurred to him that the house was very quiet and he put his head round the door and shouted up the stairs. When he got no reply he went up and found the bed unmade, the bathroom still warm and wet with steam, and Maureen's everyday hat and coat lying on a chair with her familiar brown handbag on it. Bertram came down, examined the rest of the house, then went on out into the garden. Maureen had been doing the laundry before breakfast. There was linen, almost dry, on the clothesline and a basket lying on the grass under it, but that was all. The little rectangle of land was quite empty."

As his deep voice ceased, he gave Campion a sidelong glance.

"And that, my lad, is that," he said. "Neither Peter nor Maureen has been seen since. When they didn't show up, Bertram consulted the rest of the family and after waiting for two days, they went to the police."

"Really?" Mr. Campion was fascinated in spite of himself. "Is that *all* you've got?"

"Not quite but the rest is hardly helpful." Luke sounded almost gratified. "Wherever they are, they're not in the house or garden. If they walked out they did it without being seen—which is more of a feat than you'd expect because they had interested relatives and friends all round them—and the only things that anyone is sure they took with them are a couple of clean linen sheets. 'Fine winding sheets,' one lady called them."

Mr. Campion's brows rose behind his big spectacles.

"That's a delicate touch," he said. "I take it there is no suggestion of foul play?"

"Foul play is becoming positively common in London. I don't know what the old Town is coming to," Luke said gloomily, "but this setup sounds healthy and happy enough. The McGills seem to have been pleasant normal young people and yet there are one or two little items which make one wonder. As far as we can find out, Peter was not on his usual train to the City that morning, but we have one witness—a third cousin of his—who says she followed him up the street from his house to the corner just as she often did on weekday mornings. At the top of the street she went one way and she assumed that as usual he went the other, but no one else seems to have seen him and she's probably mistaken. Well, now, here we are. Stand here for a minute."

He had paused on the pavement of a narrow residential street, shady with plane trees and lined with pairs of pleasant little houses, stone-dashed and bay-windowed, in a style which is now a little out of fashion.

"The next gate along here belongs to the Heskiths," he went on, lowering his voice a tone or so. "We'll walk rather quickly past there because we don't want any more help from Bertram at the moment. He's a good enough chap but he sees himself as the watchdog of his sister-in-law's property and the way he follows me round makes me self-conscious. His house is Number 25—the odd numbers are on this side—29 is two doors along. Now Number 31, which is actually adjoined to 29 on the other side, is closed. The old lady who owns it is in the hospital; but in 33 there live two sisters who are aunts of Peter's. They moved there soon after the young couple.

"One is a widow," Luke sketched a portly juglike silhouette with his hands, "and the other is a spinster who looks like two yards of pumpwater. Both are very interested in their nephew and his wife but whereas the widow is prepared to take a more or less benevolent view of her young relations, the spinster, Miss Dove, is apt to be critical. She told me Maureen didn't know how to budget her money and I think that from time to time she'd had a few words with the girl on the subject. I heard about the 'fine linen sheets' from her. Apparently she'd told Maureen off about buying something so expensive but the young bride had saved up for them and she'd got them."

Luke sighed. "Women are like that," he said. "They get a yen for something and they want it and that's all there is to it. Miss Dove says she watched Maureen hanging them out on the line early in the morning of the day she vanished. There's one upstairs window in her house from which she can just see part of the garden at 29 if she stands on a chair and clings to the sash."

He grinned. "She happened to be doing just that at about half-past six on the day the McGills disappeared and she insists she saw them hanging there—the sheets, I mean. She recognized them by the crochet on the top edge. They're certainly not in the house now. Miss Dove hints delicately that I should search Bertram's home for them!"

Mr. Campion's pale eyes had narrowed and his mouth was smiling.

"It's a honey of a story," he murmured. "A sort of circumstantial history of the utterly impossible. The whole thing just can't have happened. How very odd, Charles. Did anybody else see Maureen that morning? Could she have walked out of the front door and come up the street with the linen over her arm unnoticed? I am not asking *would* she but *could* she?"

"No." Luke made no bones about it. "Even had she wanted to, which is unlikely, it's virtually impossible. There are the cousins opposite, you see. They live in the house with the red geraniums over there, directly in front of Number 29. They are some sort of distant relatives of Peter's. A father, mother, five marriageable daughters—it was one of them who says she followed Peter up the road that morning. Also there's an old Irish granny who sits up in bed in the window of the front room all day. She's not very reliable—for instance, she can't remember if Peter came out of the house at his usual time that day—but she would have noticed if Maureen had done so. No one saw Maureen that morning except Miss Dove, who, as I told you, watched her hanging linen on the line. The paper comes early;

the milkman heard her washing machine from the scullery door when he left his bottles but he did not see her."

"What about the postman?"

"He's no help. He's a new man on the round and can't even remember if he called at 29. It's a long street and, as he says, the houses are all alike. He gets to 29 about 7:25 and seldom meets anybody at that hour. He wouldn't know the McGills if he saw them anyhow. Come on in, Campion—take a look round and see what you think."

Mr. Campion followed his friend up a narrow garden path to where a uniformed officer stood on guard before the front door. He was aware of a flutter behind the curtains in the house opposite and a tall, thin woman with a determinedly blank expression walked down the path of the next house but one and bowed to Luke meaningly as she paused at her gate before going back.

"Miss Dove," said Luke unnecessarily, as he opened the door of Number 29 Chestnut Grove.

The house had few surprises for Mr. Campion. It was almost exactly as he had imagined it. The furniture in the hall and front room was new and sparse, leaving plenty of room for future acquisitions; the kitchen-dining-room was well lived in and conveyed a distinct personality. Someone without much money, but who liked nice things, had lived there. He or she—and he suspected it was a she—had been generous too, despite her economies, if the "charitable" calendars and packets of gypsy pegs bought at the door were any guide. The breakfast table had been left exactly as Bertram Heskith had found it and his cup was still there.

The thin man in the hornrimmed glasses wandered through the house without comment, Luke at his heels. The scene was just as stated. There was no sign of hurried flight, no evidence of packing, no hint of violence. The dwelling was not so much untidy as in the process of being used. There was a pair of man's pajamas on the stool in the bathroom and a towel hung over the edge of the basin to dry. The woman's handbag and coat on a chair in the bedroom contained the usual miscellany and two pounds three shillings, some coppers, and a set of keys.

Mr. Campion looked at everything—the clothes hanging neatly in the cupboards, the dead flowers still in the vases; but the only item which appeared to hold his attention was the photograph of a wedding group which he found in a silver frame on the dressing table.

He stood before it for a long time apparently fascinated, yet it was not a remarkable picture. As is occasionally the case in such photographs, the two central figures were the least dominant characters in the entire group of vigorous, laughing wedding guests. Maureen, timid and gentle, with a slender figure and big dark eyes, looked positively scared of her own bridesmaid, and Peter, although solid and with a determined chin, had a panic-stricken look about him which contrasted with the cheerfully assured grin of the best man.

"That's Heskith," said Luke. "You can see the sort of chap he is—not one of nature's noblemen, but not a man to go imagining things. When he says he felt the two were there that morning, perfectly normal and happy as usual, I believe him."

"No Miss Dove here?" said Campion, still looking at the group photograph.

"No. That's her sister though, deputizing for the bride's mother. And that's the girl from opposite, the one who thinks she saw Peter go up the road."

Luke put a forefinger over the face of the third bridesmaid. "There's another sister here and the rest are cousins. I understand the pic doesn't do the bride justice. Everybody says she was a very pretty girl . . ." He corrected himself. "Is, I mean."

"The bridegroom looks like a reasonable type to me," murmured Mr. Campion. "A little apprehensive, perhaps."

"I wonder." Luke spoke thoughtfully. "The Heskiths had another photo of him and perhaps it's more marked in that—but don't you think there's a kind of ruthlessness in that face, Campion? It's not quite recklessness—more, I'd say, like decision. I knew a sergeant in the war with a face like that. He was mild enough in the ordinary way but once something shook him he acted fast and pulled no punches whatever. Well, that's neither here nor there. Come and inspect the clothesline and then, Heaven help you, you'll know as much as I do."

Luke led the way to the back and stood for a moment on the concrete path which ran under the kitchen window separating the house from the small rectangle of shorn grass which was all there was of a garden.

A high hedge and rustic fencing separated it from the neighbors on the right, and at the bottom there was a garden shed and a few fruit trees; on the left, the greenery in the neglected garden of the old lady who was in the hospital had grown up high so that a green wall screened the garden from all but the prying eyes of Miss Dove who, at that moment, Mr. Campion suspected, was standing on a chair and clinging to a sash to peer at them.

Luke indicated the empty line slung across the grass. "I had the linen brought in," he said. "The Heskiths were worrying and there seemed no earthly point in leaving it out to rot."

"What's in the shed?"

"A spade and fork and a lawn mower," said Luke promptly. "Come and look. The floor is beaten earth and if it's been disturbed in thirty years I'll eat my hat in Trafalgar Square. I suppose we'll have to dig it up in the end but we'll be wasting our time."

Mr. Campion went over and glanced into the tarred wooden hut. It was tidy and dusty and the floor was dry and hard. Outside, a dilapidated pair of steps leaned against the six-foot brick wall which marked the boundary.

Mr. Campion tried the steps gingerly. They held firmly enough, so he climbed up to look over the wall to the narrow path which separated it from the fence in the rear garden of the house in the next street.

"That's an old right of way," Luke said. "It leads down between the two residential roads. These suburban places are not very matey, you know. Half the time one street doesn't know the next. Chestnut Grove is classier than Philpott Avenue which runs parallel with it."

Mr. Campion descended and dusted his hands. He was grinning and his eyes were dancing.

"I wonder if anybody there noticed her," he said. "She must have been carrying the sheets."

Luke turned round slowly and stared at him.

"You're not suggesting she simply walked down here and over the wall and out! In the clothes she'd been washing in? It's crazy. Why should she? And did her husband go with her?"

"No, I think he went down Chestnut Grove as usual, doubled back down this path as soon as he came to the other end of it near the station, picked up his wife, and went off with her through Philpott Avenue to the bus stop. They'd only have to get to Broadway to find a cab, you see."

Luke's dark face still wore an expression of complete incredulity.

"But for Peter's sake *why?*" he demanded. "Why clear out in the middle of breakfast on a washday morning? And why take the sheets? Young couples can do the most unlikely things—but there are limits, Campion! They didn't take their savings bank books, you know. There's not much in them but they're still there in the writing desk in the front room. What in the world are you getting at, Campion?"

The thin man walked slowly back to the patch of grass.

"I expect the sheets were dry and she'd folded them into the basket before breakfast," he began slowly. "As she ran out of the house they were lying there and she couldn't resist taking them with her. The husband must have been irritated with her when he saw her with them, but people are like that. When they're running from a fire they save the oddest things."

"But she wasn't running from a fire."

"Wasn't she!" Mr. Campion laughed. "Listen, Charles. If the postman called, he reached the house at 7:25. I think he did call and delivered an ordinary plain business envelope which was too commonplace for him to remember. It would be the plainest of plain envelopes. Well then: who was due at 7:30?"

"Bert Heskith. I told you."

"Exactly. So there were five minutes in which to escape. Five minutes for a determined, resourceful man like Peter McGill to act promptly. His wife was generous and easy-going, remember, and so, thanks to that decisiveness which you yourself noticed in his face, he rose to the occasion.

"He had only five minutes, Charles, to escape all those powerful personalities with their jolly, avid faces whom we saw in the wedding group. They were all living remarkably close to him—ringing him round as it were—so that it was a ticklish business to elude them. He went out the front way so that the kindly watchful eyes would see him as usual and not be alarmed.

"There wasn't time to take anything at all and it was only because Maureen, flying through the garden to escape the back way, saw the sheets in the basket and couldn't resist her treasures that she salvaged them. She wasn't quite so ruthless as Peter. She had to take something from the old life, however glistening were the prospects for . . ."

Campion broke off abruptly. Chief-Inspector Luke, with dawning comprehension in his eyes, was already halfway to the gate on the way to the nearest police telephone box.

Mr. Campion was in his own sitting room in Bottle Street, Piccadilly, later that evening when Luke called. The Chief-Inspector came in jauntily, his black eyes dancing with amusement.

"It wasn't the Football Pool but the Irish Sweep," he said. "I got the details out of the Promoters. They've been wondering what to do ever since the story broke. They're in touch with the McGills, of course, but Peter has taken every precaution to insure secrecy and he's insisting on his rights. He must have known his wife's tender heart and have made up his mind what he'd do if ever a really big win came off. The moment he got the letter telling him of his luck he put the plan into action."

Luke paused and shook his head admiringly. "I have to hand it to him," he said. "Seventy-five thousand pounds is like a nice fat chicken—plenty and more for two but only a taste for a very big family."

"What will you do?"

"Us? The police? Oh, officially we're baffled. We shall retire gracefully. It's not our business—strictly a family affair."

He sat down and raised the glass his host had handed to him. "Here's to the mystery of the Villa Mary Celeste," he said. "I had a blind spot for it. It foxed me completely. Good luck to them, though. You know, Campion, you had a point when you said that the really insoluble mystery is the one which no one can bring himself to spoil. What put you on to it?"

"I suspect the charm of relatives who call at seven-thirty in the morning," said Mr. Campion.

❦ | Celia Thaxter

Nearly all historians of the mystery story say that the tale of detection is dying out. They predict that the crime story will soon take over; and, of equal value, there will be development of the fact crime story. The growing interest of young people in the forensic sciences—a field that is rapidly attracting young women as well as men—could indicate the validity of this projection. But there are many other reasons for future development. Stories about crime often take the form of social protest. As Julian Symons, a historian of the mystery and crime story, points out, such stories can flourish only in a liberal air. The Nazis and the Russians—despite the fact that Dostoevski wrote the greatest of all crime novels, *Crime and Punishment*—considered them decadent, and of course true crime stories revealed far too much about society to be tolerated.

One of the first true crime historians was a woman, Celia Thaxter, who appeared an unlikely candidate for such an innovative role. She had been reared on an attractive group of islands off the coast of New Hampshire, a favorite resort for New England writers. She became a well-known nineteenth-century poet and fine essayist, but with her publication of *A Memorable Murder* she became a household name. She wrote the story in good faith, but because she was a woman she had to ask constant reassurance that she had not "offended against the good taste" or "proprieties of existence," because "the subject was a delicate one to handle, so notorious, so ghastly and dreadful!" The literary lights of the period roared their approval. Laurence Hutton called *A Memorable Murder* "one of the most vivid bits of prose in American literature," and John Greenleaf Whittier wrote to her:

"I often think of you in connection with the island tragedy. The imagination of man never conceived anything more dreadful than its grim reality. What a weird, awful interest will for all time vest that island."

Often retold by more contemporary writers, the best version is still Celia Thaxter's.

A Memorable Murder

At the Isles of Shoals, on the 5th of March in the year 1873, occurred one of the most monstrous tragedies ever enacted on this planet. The sickening details of the double murder are well known; the newspapers teemed with them for months: but the pathos of the story is not realized; the world does not know how gentle a life these poor people led, how innocently happy were their quiet days. They were all Norwegians. The more I see of the natives of this far-off land, the more I admire the fine qualities which seem to characterize them as a race. Gentle, faithful, intelligent, God-fearing human beings, they daily use such courtesy toward each other and all who come in contact with them, as puts our ruder Yankee manners to shame. The men and women living on this lonely island were like the sweet, honest, simple folk we read of in Bjornson's charming Norwegian stories, full of kindly thoughts and ways. The murdered Anethe might have been the Eli of Bjornson's beautiful *Arne* or the Ragnhild of Boyesen's lovely romance. They rejoiced to find a home just such as they desired in this peaceful place; the women took such pleasure in the little house which they kept so neat and bright, in their flock of hens, their little dog Ringe, and all their humble belongings! The Norwegians are an exceptionally affectionate people; family ties are very strong and precious among them. Let me tell the story of their sorrow as simply as may be.

Louis Wagner murdered Anethe and Karen Christensen at midnight on the 5th of March, two years ago this spring. The whole affair shows the calmness of a practiced hand; *there was no malice in the deed,* no heat; it was one of the coolest instances of deliberation ever chronicled in the annals of crime. He admits that these people had shown him nothing but kindness. He says in so many words, "They were my best friends." They looked upon him as a brother. Yet he did not hesitate to murder them. The island called Smutty-Nose by human perversity (since in old times it bore the pleasanter title of Haley's Island) was selected to be the scene of this disaster. Long ago I lived two years upon it, and know well its whitened ledges and grassy slopes, its low thickets of wild-rose and bayberry, its sea-wall still intact, connecting it with the small island Malaga, opposite Appledore, and the ruined break-water which links it with Cedar Island on the other side. A lonely cairn, erected by some long ago forgotten fishermen or sailors, stands upon the highest rock at the southeastern extremity; at its western end a few houses are scattered, small, rude dwellings, with the square old Haley house near; two or three fish-houses are falling into decay about the water-side, and the ancient wharf drops stone by stone into the little cove, where every day the tide ebbs and flows and ebbs again with pleasant sound and freshness. Near the houses is a small grave-yard, where a few of the natives sleep, and not far, the graves of the fourteen Spaniards lost in the wreck of the ship *Sagunto* in the year 1813. I used to think it was a pleasant place, that low, rocky, and grassy island, though so wild and lonely.

From the little town of Laurvig, near Christiania, in Norway, came John and Maren Hontvet to this country, and five years ago took up their abode in this desolate spot, in one of the cottages facing the cove and Appledore. And there they lived through the long winters and the lovely summers, John making a comfortable living by fishing, Maren, his wife, keeping as bright and tidy and sweet a little home for him as man could desire. The bit of garden they cultivated in the summer was a pleasure to them; they made their house as pretty as they could with paint and paper and gay pictures, and Maren had a shelf for her plants at the window; and John was always so good to her, so kind and thoughtful of her comfort and of what would please her, she was entirely happy. Sometimes she was a little lonely, perhaps, when he was tossing afar off on the sea, setting or hauling his trawls, or had sailed to Portsmouth to sell his fish. So that she was doubly glad when the news came that some of her people were coming over from Norway to live with her. And first, in the month of May, 1871, came her sister Karen, who stayed only a short time with Maren, and then came to Appledore, where she lived at service two years, till within a fortnight of her death. The first time I saw Maren, she brought her sister to us, and I was charmed with the little woman's beautiful behavior; she was so gentle, courteous, decorous, she left on my mind a most delightful impression. Her face struck me as remarkably good and intelligent, and her gray eyes were full of light.

Karen was a rather sad-looking woman, about twenty-nine years old; she had lost a lover in Norway long since, and in her heart she fretted and mourned for this continually: she could not speak a word of English at first, but went patiently about her work and soon learned enough, and proved herself an excellent servant, doing faithfully and thoroughly everything she undertook, as is the way of her people generally. Her personal neatness was most attractive. She wore gowns made of cloth woven by herself in Norway, a coarse blue stuff, always neat and clean, and often I used to watch her as she sat by the fire spinning at a spinning-wheel brought from her own country; she made such a pretty picture, with her blue gown and fresh white apron, and the nice, clear white muslin bow with which she was in the habit of fastening her linen collar, that she was very agreeable to look upon. She had a pensive way of letting her head droop a little sideways as she spun, and while the low wheel hummed monotonously, she would sit crooning sweet, sad old Norwegian airs by the hour together, perfectly unconscious that she was affording such pleasure to a pair of appreciative eyes. On the 12th of October, 1872, in the second year of her stay with us, her brother, Ivan Christensen, and his wife, Anethe Mathea, came over from their Norseland in an evil day, and joined Maren and John at their island, living in the same house with them.

Ivan and Anethe had been married only since Christmas of the preceding year. Ivan was tall, light-haired, rather quiet and grave. Anethe was young, fair, and merry, with thick, bright sunny hair, which was so long it reached, when unbraided, nearly to her knees; blue-eyed, with brilliant teeth and clear, fresh complexion, beautiful, and beloved beyond expression by her young husband, Ivan. Mathew Hontvet, John's brother, had also joined the little circle a year before, and now Maren's happiness was complete. Delighted to welcome them all, she made all things pleasant for them, and she told me only a few days ago, "I never was so happy in my life as when we were all living there together." So they abode in peace and quiet, with not an evil thought in their minds, kind and considerate toward each other, the men devoted to their women and the women repaying them with interest, till out of the perfectly cloudless sky one day a bolt descended, without a whisper of warning, and brought ruin and desolation into that peaceful home.

Louis Wagner, who had been in this country seven years, appeared at the Shoals two years before the date of the murder. He lived about the islands during that time. He was born in Ueckermünde, a small town of lower Pomerania, in Northern

Prussia. Very little is known about him, though there were vague rumors that his past life had not been without difficulties, and he had boasted foolishly among his mates that "not many had done what he had done and got off in safety"; but people did not trouble themselves about him or his past, all having enough to do to earn their bread and keep the wolf from the door. Maren describes him as tall, powerful, dark, with a peculiarly quiet manner. She says she never saw him drunk— he seemed always anxious to keep his wits about him: he would linger on the outskirts of a drunken brawl, listening to and absorbing everything, but never mixing himself up in any disturbance. He was always lurking in corners, lingering, looking, listening, and he would look no man straight in the eyes. She spoke, however, of having once heard him disputing with some sailors, at table, about some point of navigation; she did not understand it, but all were against Louis, and, waxing warm, all strove to show him he was in the wrong. As he rose and left the table she heard him mutter to himself with an oath, "I know I'm wrong, but I'll never give in!" During the winter preceding the one in which his hideous deed was committed, he lived at Star Island and fished alone, in a wherry; but he made very little money, and came often over to the Hontvets, where Maren gave him food when he was suffering from want, and where he received always a welcome and the utmost kindness. In the following June he joined Hontvet in his business of fishing, and took up his abode as one of the family at Smutty-Nose. During the summer he was "crippled," as he said, by the rheumatism, and they were all very good to him, and sheltered, fed, nursed, and waited upon him the greater part of the season. He remained with them five weeks after Ivan and Anethe arrived, so that he grew to know Anethe as well as Maren, and was looked upon as a brother by all of them, as I have said before. Nothing occurred to show his true character, and in November he left the island and the kind people whose hospitality he was to repay so fearfully, and going to Portsmouth he took passage in another fishing schooner, the *Addison Gilbert*, which was presently wrecked off the coast, and he was again thrown out of employment. Very recklessly he said to Waldemar Ingebertsen, to Charles Jonsen, and even to John Hontvet himself, at different times, that "he must have money if he murdered for it." He loafed about Portsmouth eight weeks, doing nothing. Meanwhile Karen left our service in February, intending to go to Boston and work at a sewing machine, for she was not strong and thought she should like it better than housework, but before going she lingered awhile with her sister Maren—fatal delay for her! Maren told me that during this time Karen went to Portsmouth and had her teeth removed, meaning to provide herself with a new set. At the Jonsens' where Louis was staying, one day she spoke to Mrs. Jonsen of her mouth, that it was so sensitive since the teeth had been taken out; and Mrs. Jonsen asked her how long she must wait before the new set could be put in. Karen replied that it would be three months. Louis Wagner was walking up and down at the other end of the room with his arms folded, his favorite attitude. Mrs. Jonsen's daughter passed near him and heard him mutter, "Three months! What is the use! In three months you will be dead!" He did not know the girl was so near, and turning, he confronted her. He knew she must have heard what he said, and he glared at her like a wild man.

On the fifth day of March, 1873, John Hontvet, his brother Mathew, and Ivan Christensen set sail in John's little schooner, the *Clara Bella*, to draw their trawls. At that time four of the islands were inhabited: one family on White Island, at the light-house; the workmen who were building the new hotel on Star Island, and one or two households beside; the Hontvet family at Smutty-Nose; and on Appledore, the household at the large house, and on the southern side, opposite Smutty-Nose, a little cottage, where lived Jörge Edvardt Ingebertsen, his wife and children, and several men who fished with him. Smutty-Nose is not in sight of the large house at Appledore, so we were in ignorance of all that happened on that dreadful night, longer than the other inhabitants of the Shoals.

John, Ivan, and Mathew went to draw their trawls, which had been set some miles to the eastward of the islands. They intended to be back to dinner, and then to go on to Portsmouth with their fish, and bait the trawls afresh, ready to bring back to set again next day. But the wind was strong and fair for Portsmouth and ahead for the islands; it would have been a long beat home against it; so they went on to Portsmouth, without touching at the island to leave one man to guard the women, as had been their custom. This was the first night in all the years Maren had lived there that the house was without a man to protect it. But John, always thoughtful for her, asks Emil Ingebertsen, whom he met on the fishing-grounds, to go over from Appledore and tell her that they had gone on to Portsmouth with the favoring wind, but that they hoped to be back that night. And he would have been back had the bait he expected from Boston arrived on the train in which it was due. How curiously everything adjusted itself to favor the bringing about of this horrible catastrophe! The bait did not arrive till the half past twelve train, and they were obliged to work the whole night getting their trawls ready, thus leaving the way perfectly clear for Louis Wagner's awful work.

The three women left alone watched and waited in vain for the schooner to return, and kept the dinner hot for the men, and patiently wondered why they did not come. In vain they searched the wide horizon for that returning sail. Ah me, what pathos is in that longing look of women's eyes for far-off sails! that gaze so eager, so steadfast, that it would almost seem as if it must conjure up the ghostly shape of glimmering canvas from the mysterious distances of sea and sky, and draw it unerringly home by the mere force of intense wistfulness! And those gentle eyes, that were never to see the light of another sun, looked anxiously across the heaving sea till twilight fell, and then John's messenger, Emil, arrived—Emil Ingebertsen, courteous and gentle as a youthful knight—and reassured them with his explanation, which having given, he departed, leaving them in a much more cheerful state of mind. So the three sisters, with only the little dog Ringe for a protector, sat by the fire chatting together cheerfully. They fully expected the schooner back again that night from Portsmouth, but they were not ill at ease while they waited. Of what should they be afraid? They had not an enemy in the world! No shadow crept to the fireside to warn them what was at hand, no portent of death chilled the air as they talked their pleasant talk and made their little plans in utter unconsciousness. Karen was to have gone to Portsmouth with the fishermen that day; she was all ready dressed to go. Various little commissions were given her, errands to do for the two sisters she was to leave behind. Maren wanted some buttons, and "I'll give you one for a pattern; I'll put it in your purse," she said to Karen, "and then when you open your purse you'll be sure to remember it." (That little button, of a peculiar pattern, was found in Wagner's possession afterward.) They sat up till ten o'clock, talking together. The night was bright and calm; it was a comfort to miss the bitter winds that had raved about the little dwelling all the long, rough winter. Already it was spring; this calm was the first token of its coming. It was the 5th of March; in a few weeks the weather would soften, the grass grow green, and Anethe would see the first flowers in this strange country so far from her home where she had left father and mother, kith and kin, for love of Ivan. The delicious days of summer at hand would transform the work of the toiling fishermen to pleasure, and all things would bloom and smile about the poor people on the lonely rock! Alas, it was not to be.

At ten o'clock they went to bed. It was cold and "lonesome" upstairs, so Maren put some chairs by the side of the lounge, laid a mattress upon it, and made up a bed for Karen in the kitchen, where she presently fell asleep. Maren and Anethe slept in the next room. So safe they felt themselves, they did not pull down a curtain, nor even try to fasten the house-door. They went to their rest in absolute security and perfect trust. It was the first still night of the new year; a young moon stole softly down toward the west, a gentle wind breathed through the quiet dark, and the waves whispered gently about the island, helping to lull those innocent souls to yet more peaceful slumber. Ah, where were the gales of March that might have plowed that tranquil sea to foam, and cut off the fatal path of Louis Wagner to that happy home! But nature seeemed to pause and wait for him. I remember looking abroad over the waves that night and rejoicing over "the first calm night of the year!" It was so still, so bright! The hope of all the light and beauty a few weeks would bring forth stirred me to sudden joy. There should be spring again after the long winter-weariness.

> "Can trouble live in April days,
> Or sadness in the summer moons?"

I thought, as I watched the clear sky, grown less hard than it had been for weeks, and sparkling with stars. But before another sunset it seemed to me that beauty had fled out of the world, and that goodness, innocence, mercy, gentleness, were a mere mockery of empty words.

Here let us leave the poor women, asleep on the lonely rock, with no help near them in heaven or upon earth, and follow the fishermen to Portsmouth, where they arrived about four o'clock that afternoon. One of the first men whom they saw as they neared the town was Louis Wagner; to him they threw the rope from the schooner, and he helped draw her in to the wharf. Greetings passed between them; he spoke to Mathew Hontvet, and as he looked at Ivan Christensen, the men noticed a flush pass over Louis's face. He asked were they going out again that night? Three times before they parted he asked that question; he saw that all the three men belonging to the island had come away together; he began to realize his opportunity. They answered him that if their bait came by the train in which they expected it, they hoped to get back that night, but if it was late they should be obliged to stay till morning, baiting their trawls; and they asked him to come and help them. It is a long and tedious business, the baiting of trawls; often more than a thousand hooks are to be manipulated, and lines and hooks coiled, clear of tangles, into tubs, all ready for throwing overboard when the fishing-grounds are reached. Louis gave them a half promise that he would help them, but they did not see him again after leaving the wharf. The three fishermen were hungry, not having touched at their island, where Maren always provided them with a supply of food to take with them; they asked each other if either had brought any money with which to buy bread, and it came out that every one had left his pocketbook at home. Louis, standing by, heard all this. He asked John, then, if he had made fishing pay. John answered that he had cleared about six hundred dollars.

The men parted, the honest three about their business; but Louis, what became of him with his evil thoughts? At about half past seven he went into a liquor shop and had a glass of something; not enough to make him unsteady,—he was too wise for that. He was not seen again in Portsmouth by any human creature that night. He must have gone, after that, directly down to the river, that beautiful, broad river, the Piscataqua, upon whose southern bank the quaint old city of Portsmouth dreams its quiet days away; and there he found a boat ready to his hand, a dory belonging to a man by the name of David Burke, who had that day furnished it with new tholepins. When it was picked up afterward off the mouth of the river, Louis's anxious oars had eaten half-way through the substance of these pins, which are always made of the hardest, toughest wood that can be found. A terrible piece of rowing must that have been, in one night! Twelve miles from the city to the Shoals,—three to the light-houses, where the river meets the open sea, nine more to the islands; nine back again to Newcastle next morning! He took that boat, and with the favoring tide dropped down the rapid river where the swift current is so strong that oars are scarcely needed, except to keep the boat steady. Truly all nature seemed to play into his hands; this first relenting night of earliest spring favored him with its stillness, the tide was fair, the wind was fair, the little moon gave him just enough light, without betraying him to any curious eyes, as he glided down the three miles between the river banks, in haste to reach the sea. Doubtless the light west wind played about him as delicately as if he had been the most human of God's creatures; nothing breathed remonstrance in his ear, nothing whispered in the whispering water that rippled about his inexorable keel, steering straight for the Shoals through the quiet darkness. The snow lay thick and white upon the land in the moonlight; lamps twinkled here and there from dwellings on either side; in Eliot and Newcastle, in Portsmouth and Kittery, roofs, chimneys, and gables showed faintly in the vague light; the leafless trees clustered dark in hollows or lifted their tracery of bare boughs in higher spaces against the wintry sky. His eyes must have looked on it all, whether he saw the peaceful picture or not. Beneath many a humble roof honest folk were settling into their untroubled rest, as "this planned piece of deliberate wickedness" was stealing silently by with his heart full of darkness, blacker than the black tide that swirled beneath his boat and bore him fiercely on. At the river's mouth stood the sentinel light-houses, sending their great spokes of light afar into the night, like the arms of a wide humanity stretching into the darkness helping hands to bring all who needed succor safely home. He passed them, first the tower at Fort Point, then the taller one at Whale's Back, steadfastly holding aloft their warning fires. There was no signal from the warning bell as he rowed by, though a danger more subtle, more deadly, than fog, or hurricane, or pelting storm was passing swift beneath it. Unchallenged by anything in earth or heaven, he kept on his way and gained the great outer ocean, doubtless pulling strong and steadily, for he had no time to lose, and the longest night was all too short for an undertaking such as this. Nine miles from the light-houses to the islands! Slowly he makes his way; it seems to take an eternity of time. And now he is midway between the islands and the coast. That little toy of a boat with its one occupant in the midst of the awful, black, heaving sea! The vast dim ocean whispers with a thousand waves; against the boat's side the ripples lightly tap, and pass and are lost; the air is full of fine, mysterious voices of winds and waters. Has he no fear, alone there on the midnight sea with such a purpose in his heart? The moonlight sends a long, golden track across the waves; it touches his dark face and figure, it glitters on his dripping oars. On his right hand Boone Island light shows like a setting star on the horizon, low on his left the two beacons twinkle off Newburyport, at the mouth of the Merrimack River; all the light-houses stand watching along the coast, wheeling their long, slender shafts of radiance as if pointing at this black atom creeping over the face of the planet with such colossal evil in his heart. Before him glitters the Shoals' light at White Island, and helps to guide him to his prey. Alas, my friendly light-house, that you should serve so terrible a purpose! Steadily the oars click in the rowlocks; stroke after stroke of the broad blades draws him away from the lessening line of land, over the wavering floor of the ocean, nearer the lonely rocks. Slowly the coast-lights fade, and now the rote of the sea among the lonely ledges of the Shoals salutes his attentive ear. A little longer and he nears Appledore, the first island, and now he passed by the snow-covered, ice-bound rock, with the long buildings showing clear in the moonlight. He must have looked at them as he went past. I wonder we who slept beneath the roofs that glimmered to his eyes in the uncertain light did not feel, through the thick veil of sleep, what fearful thing passed by! But we slumbered peacefully as the unhappy women whose doom every click of those oars in the rowlocks, like the ticking of some dreadful clock, was bringing nearer and nearer. Between the islands he passes; they are full of chilly gleams and glooms. There is no scene more weird than these snow-covered rocks in winter, more shudderful and strange: the moonlight touching them with mystic glimmer, the black water breaking about them and the vast shadowy spaces of the sea stretching to the horizon on every side, full of vague sounds, of half lights and shadows, of fear, and of mystery. The island he seeks lies before him, lone and still; there is no gleam in any window, there is no help near, nothing upon which the women can call for succor. He does not land in the cove where all boats put in, he rows round to the south side and draws his boat up on the rocks. His red returning footsteps are found here next day, staining the snow. He makes his way to the house he knows so well.

All is silent: nothing moves, nothing sounds but the hushed voices of the sea. His hand is on the latch, he enters stealthily, there is nothing to resist him. The little dog, Ringe, begins to bark sharp and loud, and Karen rouses, crying, "John, is that you?" thinking the expected fishermen had returned. Louis seizes a chair and strikes at her in the dark; the clock on the shelf above her head falls down with the jarring of the blow, and stops at exactly seven minutes to one. Maren in the next room, waked suddenly from her sound sleep, trying in vain to make out the meaning of it all, cries, "What's the matter?" Karen answers, "John scared me!" Maren springs from her bed and tries to open her chamber door; Louis has fastened it on the other side by pushing a stick through over the latch. With her heart leaping with terror the poor child shakes the door with all her might, in vain. Utterly confounded and bewildered, she hears Karen screaming, "John kills me! John kills me!" She hears the sound of repeated blows and shrieks, till at last her sister falls heavily against the door, which gives way, and Maren rushes out. She catches dimly a glimpse of a tall figure outlined against the southern window; she seizes poor Karen and drags her with the strength of frenzy within the bedroom. This unknown terror, this fierce, dumb monster who never utters a sound to betray himself through the whole, pursues her with blows, strikes her three times with a chair, either blow with fury sufficient to kill her, had it been light enough for him to see how to direct it; but she gets her sister inside and the door shut, and holds it against him with all her might and Karen's failing strength. What a little heroine was this poor child, struggling with the force of desperation to save herself and her sisters!

All this time Anethe lay dumb, not daring to move or breathe, roused from the deep sleep of youth and health by this nameless, formless terror. Maren, while she strives to hold the door at which Louis rattles again and again, calls to her in anguish, "Anethe, Anethe! Get out of the window! run! hide!" The poor girl, almost paralyzed with fear, tries to obey, puts her bare feet out of the low window, and stands outside in the freezing snow, with one light garment over her cowering figure, shrinking in the cold winter wind, the clear moonlight touching her white face and bright hair and fair young shoulders. "Scream! scream!" shouts frantic Maren. "Somebody at Star Island may hear!" but Anethe answers with the calmness of despair, "I cannot make a sound." Maren screams, herself, but the feeble sound avails nothing. "Run! run!" she cries to Anethe; but again Anethe answers, "I cannot move."

Louis has left off trying to force the door; he listens. Are the women trying to escape? He goes out-of-doors. Maren flies to the window; he comes round the corner of the house and confronts Anethe where she stands in the snow. The moonlight shines full in his face; she shrieks loudly and distinctly, "Louis, Louis!" Ah, he is discovered, he is recognized! Quick as thought he goes back to the front door, at the side of which stands an ax, left there by Maren, who had used it the day before to cut the ice from the well. He returns to Anethe standing shuddering there. It is no matter that she is beautiful, young, and helpless to resist, that she has been kind to him, that she never did a human creature harm, that she stretches her gentle hands out to him in agonized entreaty, crying piteously, "Oh, Louis, Louis, Louis!" He raises the ax and brings it down on her bright head in one tremendous blow, and she sinks without a sound and lies in a heap, with her warm blood reddening the snow. Then he deals her blow after blow, almost within reach of Maren's hands, as she stands at the window. Distracted, Maren strives to rouse poor Karen, who kneels with her head on the side of the bed; with desperate entreaty she tries to get her up and away, but Karen moans, "I cannot, I cannot." She is too far gone; and then Maren knows she cannot save her, and that she must flee herself or die. So, while Louis again enters the house, she seizes a skirt and wraps it round her shoulders, and makes her way out of the open window, over Anethe's murdered body, barefooted, flying away, anywhere, breathless, shaking with terror.

Where can she go? Her little dog, frightened into silence, follows her,—pressing so close to her feet that she falls over him more than once. Looking back she sees Louis has lit a lamp and is seeking for her. She flies to the cove; if she can but find his boat and row away in it and get help! It is not there; there is no boat in which she can get away. She hears Karen's wild screams,—he is killing her! Oh where can she go? Is there any place on that little island where he will not find her? She thinks she will creep into one of the empty old houses by the water; but no, she reflects, if I hide there, Ringe will bark and betray me the moment Louis comes to look for me. And Ringe saved her life, for next day Louis's bloody tracks were found all about those old buildings where he had sought her. She flies, with Karen's awful cries in her ears, away over rocks and snow to the farthest limit she can gain. The moon has set; it is about two o'clock in the morning, and oh, so cold! She shivers and shudders from head to feet, but her agony of terror is so great she is hardly conscious of bodily sensation. And welcome is the freezing snow, the jagged ice and iron rocks that tear her unprotected feet, the bitter brine that beats against the shore, the winter winds that make her shrink and tremble; "they are not so unkind as man's ingratitude!" Falling often, rising, struggling on with feverish haste, she makes her way to the very edge of the water; down almost into the sea she creeps, between two rocks, upon her hands and knees, and crouches, face downward, with Ringe nestled close beneath her breast, not daring to move through the long hours that must pass before the sun will rise again. She is so near the ocean she can almost reach the water with her hand. Had the wind breathed the least roughly the waves must have washed over her. There let us leave her and go back to Louis Wagner. Maren heard her sister Karen's shrieks as she fled. The poor girl had crept into an unoccupied room in a distant part of the house, striving to hide herself. He could not kill her with blows, blundering in the darkness, so he wound a handkerchief about her throat and strangled her. But now he seeks anxiously for Maren. *Has* she escaped? What terror is in the thought! Escaped, to tell the tale, to accuse him as the murderer of her sisters. Hurriedly, with desperate anxiety, he seeks for her. His time was growing short; it was not in his program that this brave little creature should give him so much trouble; he had not calculated on resistance from these weak and helpless women. Already it was morning, soon it would be daylight. He could not find her in or near the house; he went down to the empty and dilapidated houses about the cove, and sought her everywhere. What a picture! That blood-stained butcher, with his dark face, crawling about those cellars, peering for that woman! He dared not spend any more time; he must go back for the money he hoped to find, his reward for this! All about the house he searches, in bureau drawers, in trunks and boxes: he finds fifteen dollars for his night's work! Several hundreds were lying between some sheets folded at the bottom of a drawer where he looked. But he cannot stop for more thorough investigation; a dreadful haste pursues him like a thousand fiends. He drags Anethe's stiffening body into the house, and leaves it on the kitchen floor. If the thought crosses his mind to set fire to the house and burn up his two victims, he dares not do it: it will make a fatal bonfire to light his homeward way; besides, it is useless, for Maren has escaped to accuse him, and the time presses so horribly! But how cool a monster is he! After all this hard work he must have refreshment to support him in the long row back to the land; knife and fork, cup and plate, were found next morning on the table near where Anethe lay; fragments of food which was not cooked in the house, but brought from Portsmouth, were scattered about. Tidy Maren had left neither dishes nor food when they went to bed. The handle of the teapot which she had left on the stove was stained and smeared with blood. Can the human mind conceive of such hideous *nonchalance?* Wagner sat down in that room and ate and drank. It is almost beyond belief! Then he went to the well with a basin and towels, tried to wash off the blood, and left towels and basin in the well. He knows he must be gone! It is certain death to linger. He takes his boat and rows away toward the dark coast and the twinkling lights; it is for dear life, now! What powerful strokes send the small skiff rushing over the water!

There is no longer any moon, the night is far spent; already the east changes, the stars fade; he rows like a madman to reach the land, but a blush of morning is stealing up the sky and sunrise is rosy over shore and sea, when panting, trembling, weary, a creature accursed, a blot on the face of the day, he lands at Newcastle—too late! Too late! In vain he casts the dory adrift; she will not float away; the flood tide bears her back to give her testimony against him, and afterward she is found at Jaffrey's Point, near the "Devil's Den," and the fact of her worn tholepins noted. Wet, covered with ice from the spray which has flown from his eager oars, utterly exhausted, he creeps to a knoll and reconnoiters; he thinks he is unobserved, and crawls on towards Portsmouth. But he is seen and recognized by many persons, and his identity established beyond a doubt. He goes to the house of Mathew Jonsen, where he has been living, steals up-stairs, changes his clothes, and appears before the family, anxious, frightened, agitated, telling Jonsen he never felt so badly in his life; that he has got into trouble and is afraid he shall be taken. He cannot eat at breakfast, says "farewell forever," goes away and is shaved, and takes the train to Boston, where he provides himself with new clothes, shoes, a complete outfit, but lingering, held by fate, he cannot fly, and before night the officer's hand is on his shoulder and he is arrested.

Meanwhile poor shuddering Maren on the lonely island, by the water-side, waits till the sun is high in heaven before she dares come forth. She thinks he may be still on the island. She said to me, "I thought he must be there, dead or alive. I thought he might go crazy and kill himself after having done all that." At last she steals out. The little dog frisks before her; it is so cold her feet cling to the rocks and snow at every step, till the skin is fairly torn off. Still and frosty is the bright morning, the water lies smiling and sparkling, the hammers of the workmen building the new hotel on Star Island sound through the quiet air. Being on the side of Smutty-Nose opposite Star, she waves her skirt, and screams to attract their attention; they hear her, turn and look, see a woman waving a signal of distress, and, surprising to relate, turn tranquilly to their work again. She realizes at last there is no hope in that direction; she must go round toward Appledore in sight of the dreadful house. Passing it afar off she gives one swift glance toward it, terrified lest in the broad sunshine she may see some horrid token of last night's work; but all is still and peaceful. She notices the curtains the three had left up when they went to bed; they are now drawn down; she knows whose hand has done this, and what it hides from the light of day. Sick at heart, she makes her painful way to the northern edge of Malaga, which is connected with Smutty-Nose by the old sea-wall. She is directly opposite Appledore and the little cottage where abide her friend and countryman, Jorge Edvardt Ingebertsen, and his wife and children. Only a quarter of a mile of the still ocean separates her from safety and comfort. She sees the children playing about the door; she calls and calls. Will no one ever hear her?

Her torn feet torment her, she is sore with blows and perishing with cold. At last her voice reaches the ears of the children, who run and tell their father that some one is crying and calling; looking across, he sees the poor little figure waving her arms, takes his dory and paddles over, and with amazement recognizes Maren in her nightdress, with bare feet and streaming hair, with a cruel bruise upon her face, with wild eyes, distracted, half senseless with cold and terror. He cries, "Maren, Maren, who has done this? what is it? who is it?" and her only answer is "Louis, Louis, Louis!" as he takes her on board his boat and rows home with her as fast as he can. From her incoherent statement he learns what has happened. Leaving her in the care of his family, he comes over across the hill to the great house on Appledore. As I sit at my desk I see him pass the window, and wonder why the old man comes so fast and anxiously through the heavy snow.

Presently I see him going back again, accompanied by several of his own countrymen and others of our workmen, carrying guns. They are going to Smutty-Nose, and take arms, thinking it possible Wagner may yet be there. I call downstairs, "What has happened?" and am answered, "Some trouble at Smutty-Nose; we hardly understand." "Probably a drunken brawl of the reckless fishermen who may have landed there," I say to myself, and go on with my work. In another half-hour I see the men returning, reinforced by others, coming fast, confusedly; and suddenly a wail of anguish comes up from the women below. I cannot believe it when I hear them crying, "Karen is dead! Anethe is dead! Louis Wagner has murdered them both!" I run out into the servants' quarters; there are all the men assembled, an awe-stricken crowd. Old Ingebertsen comes forward and tells me the bare facts, and how Maren lies at his house, half crazy, suffering with her torn and frozen feet. Then the men are dispatched to search Appledore, to find if by any chance the murderer might be concealed about the place, and I go over to Maren to see if I can do anything for her. I find the women and children with frightened faces at the little cottage; as I go into the room where Maren lies, she catches my hands, crying, "Oh, I so glad to see you! I so glad I save my life!" and with her dry lips she tells me all the story as I have told it here. Poor little creature, holding me with those wild, glittering, dilated eyes, she cannot tell me rapidly enough the whole horrible tale. Upon her cheek is yet the blood-stain from the blow he struck her with a chair, and she shows me two more upon her shoulder, and her torn feet. I go back for arnica with which to bathe them. What a mockery seems to me the "jocund day" as I emerge into the sunshine, and looking across the space of blue, sparkling water, see the house wherein all that horror lies!

Oh, brightly shines the morning sun and glitters on the white sails of the little vessel that comes dancing back from Portsmouth before the favoring wind, with the two husbands on board! How glad they are for the sweet morning and the fair wind that brings them home again! And Ivan sees in fancy Anethe's face all beautiful with welcoming smiles, and John knows how happy his good and faithful Maren will be to see him back again. Alas, how little they dream what lies before them! From Appledore they are signaled to come ashore, and Ivan and Mathew, landing, hear a confused rumor of trouble from tongues that hardly can frame the words that must tell the dreadful truth. Ivan only understands that something is wrong. His one thought is for Anethe; he flies to Ingebertsen's cottage, she may be there; he rushes in like a maniac, crying, "Anethe, Anethe! Where is Anethe?" and broken-hearted Maren answers her brother, "Anethe is—at home." He does not wait for another word, but seizes the little boat and lands at the same time with John on Smutty-Nose; with head-long haste they reach the house, other men accompanying them; ah, there are blood-stains all about the snow! Ivan is the first to burst open the door and enter. What words can tell it! There upon the floor, naked, stiff, and stark, is the woman he idolizes, for whose dear feet he could not make life's ways smooth and pleasant enough—stone dead! Dead—horribly butchered! her bright hair stiff with blood, the fair head that had so often rested on his breast crushed, cloven, mangled with the brutal ax! Their eyes are blasted by the intolerable sight: both John and Ivan stagger out and fall, senseless, in the snow. Poor Ivan! his wife a thousand times adored, the dear girl he had brought from Norway, the good, sweet girl who loved him so, whom he could not cherish tenderly enough! And he was not there to protect her! There was no one there to save her!

> "Did Heaven look on
> And would not take their part!"

Poor fellow, what had he done that fate should deal him such a blow as this! Dumb, blind with anguish, he made no sign.

> "What says the body when they spring
> Some monstrous torture-engine's whole
> Strength on it? No more says the soul."

Some of his pitying comrades lead him away, like one stupefied, and take him back to Appledore. John knows his wife is safe. Though stricken with horror and consumed with wrath, he is not paralyzed like poor Ivan, who had been smitten with worse than death. They find Karen's body in another part of the house, covered with blows and black in the face, strangled. They find Louis's tracks,—all the tokens of his disastrous presence,—the contents of trunks and drawers scattered about in his hasty search for the money, and, all within the house and without, blood, blood everywhere.

When I reach the cottage with the arnica for Maren, they have returned from Smutty-Nose. John, her husband, is there. He is a young man of the true Norse type, blue-eyed, fair-haired, tall and well-made, with handsome teeth and bronzed beard. Perhaps he is a little quiet and undemonstrative generally, but at this moment he is superb, kindled from head to feet, a fire-brand of woe and wrath, with eyes that flash and cheeks that burn. I speak a few words to him,—what words can meet such an occasion as this!—and having given directions about the use of the arnica, for Maren, I go away, for nothing more can be done for her, and every comfort she needs is hers. The outer room is full of men; they make way for me, and as I pass through I catch a glimpse of Ivan crouched with his arms thrown round his knees and his head bowed down between them, motionless, his attitude expressing such abandonment of despair as cannot be described. His whole person seems to shrink, as if deprecating the blow that has fallen upon him.

All day the slaughtered women lie as they were found, for nothing can be touched till the officers of the law have seen the whole. And John goes back to Portsmouth to tell his tale to the proper authorities. What a different voyage from the one he had just taken, when happy and careless he was returning to the home he had left so full of peace and comfort! What a load he bears back with him, as he makes his tedious way across the miles that separate him from the means of vengeance he burns to reach! But at last he arrives, tells his story, the police at other cities are at once telegraphed, and the city marshal follows Wagner to Boston. At eight o'clock that evening comes the steamer *Mayflower* to the Shoals, with all the officers on board. They land and make investigations at Smutty-Nose, then come here to Appledore and examine Maren, and, when everything is done, steam back to Portsmouth, which they reach at three o'clock in the morning. After all are gone and his awful day's work is finished at last, poor John comes back to Maren, and kneeling by the side of her bed, he is utterly overpowered with what he has passed through; he is shaken with sobs as he cries, "Oh, Maren, Maren, it is too much, too much! I cannot bear it!" And Maren throws her arms about his neck, crying, "Oh, John, John, don't! I shall be crazy, I shall die, if you go on like that." Poor innocent, unhappy people, who never wronged a fellow-creature in their lives!

But Ivan—what is their anguish to his! They dare not leave him alone lest he do himself an injury. He is perfectly mute and listless; he cannot weep, he can neither eat nor sleep. He sits like one in a horrid dream. "Oh, my poor, poor brother!" Maren cries in tones of deepest grief, when I speak his name to her next day. She herself cannot rest a moment till she hears that Louis is taken; at every sound her crazed imagination fancies he is coming back for her; she is fairly beside herself with terror and anxiety; but the night following that of the catastrophe brings us news that he is arrested, and there is stern rejoicing at the Shoals; but no vengeance taken on him can bring back those unoffending lives, or restore that gentle home. The dead are properly cared for; the blood is washed from Anethe's beautiful bright hair; she is clothed in her wedding-dress, the blue dress in which she was married, poor child, that happy Christmas time in Norway, a little more than a year ago. They are carried across the sea to Portsmouth, the burial service is read over them, and they are hidden in the earth. After poor Ivan has seen the faces of his wife and sister still and pale in their coffins, their ghastly wounds concealed as much as possible, flowers upon them and the priest praying over them, his trance of misery is broken, the grasp of despair is loosened a little about his heart. Yet hardly does he notice whether the sun shines or no, or care whether he lives or dies. Slowly his senses steady themselves from the effects of a shock that nearly destroyed him, and merciful time, with imperceptible touch, softens day by day the outlines of that picture at the memory of which he will never cease to shudder while he lives.

Louis Wagner was captured in Boston on the evening of the next day after his atrocious deed, and Friday morning, followed by a hooting mob, he was taken to the Eastern depot. At every station along the route crowds were assembled, and there were fierce cries for vengeance. At the depot in Portsmouth a dense crowd of thousands of both sexes had gathered, who assailed him with yells and curses and cries of "Tear him to pieces!" It was with difficulty he was at last safely imprisoned. Poor Maren was taken to Portsmouth from Appledore on that day. The story of Wagner's day in Boston, like every other detail of the affair, has been told by every newspaper in the country: his agitation and restlessness, noted by all who saw him; his curious, reckless talk. To one he says, "I have just killed two sailors"; to another, Jacob Toldtman, into whose shop he goes to buy shoes, "I have seen a woman lie as still as that boot," and so on. When he is caught he puts on a bold face and determines to brave it out; denies everything with tears and virtuous indignation. The men whom he has so fearfully wronged are confronted with him; his attitude is one of injured innocence; he survey them more in sorrow than in anger, while John is on fire with wrath and indignation, and hurls maledictions at him; but Ivan, poor Ivan, hurt beyond all hope or help, is utterly mute; he does not utter one word. Of what use is it to curse the murderer of his wife? It will not bring her back; he has no heart for cursing, he is too completely broken. Maren told me the first time she was brought into Louis's presence, her heart leaped so fast she could hardly breathe. She entered the room softly with her husband and Mathew Jonsen's daughter. Louis was whittling a stick. He looked up and saw her face, and the color ebbed out of his, and rushed back and stood in one burning spot in his cheek, as he looked at her and she looked at him for a space, in silence. Then he drew about his evil mind the detestable garment of sanctimoniousness, and in sentimental accents he murmured, "I'm glad Jesus loves me!" "The devil loves you!" cried John, with uncompromising veracity. "I know it wasn't nice," said decorous Maren, "but John couldn't help it; it was too much to bear!"

The next Saturday afternoon, when he was to be taken to Saco, hundreds of fishermen came to Portsmouth from all parts of the coast, determined on his destruction, and there was a fearful scene in the quiet streets of that peaceful city when he was being escorted to the train by the police and various officers of justice. Two thousand people had assembled, and such a furious, yelling crowd was never seen or heard in Portsmouth. The air was rent with cries for vengeance; showers of bricks and stones were thrown from all directions, and wounded several of the officers who surrounded Wagner. His knees trembled under him, he shook like an aspen, and the officers found it necessary to drag him along, telling him he must keep up if he would save his life. Except that they feared to injure the innocent as well as the guilty, those men would have literally torn him to pieces. But at last he was put on board the cars in safety, and carried away to prison. His demeanor throughout the term of his confinement, and during his trial and subsequent imprisonment, was a wonderful piece of acting. He really inspired people with doubt as to his guilt. I make an extract from The Portsmouth Chronicle, dated March 13, 1873: "Wagner still retains his amazing *sang froid*, which is wonderful, even in a strong-nerved German. The sympathy of most of the visitors at his jail has certainly been won by his calmness and his general appearance, which is quite prepossessing." This little instance of his method of proceeding I must subjoin: A lady who had come to converse with him on the subject of his eternal salvation said, as she left him, "I hope you put your trust in the Lord," to which he sweetly answered, "I always did, ma'am, and I always shall."

A few weeks after all this had happened, I sat by the window one afternoon, and, looking up from my work, I saw some one passing slowly,—a young man who seemed so thin, so pale, so bent and ill, that I said, "Here is some stranger who is so very sick, he is probably come to try the effect of the air, even thus early." It was Ivan Christensen. I did not recognize him. He dragged one foot after the other wearily, and walked with the feeble motion of an old man. He entered the house; his errand was to ask for work. He could not bear to go away from the neighborhood of the place where Anethe had lived and where they had been so happy, and he could not bear to work at fishing on the south side of the island, within sight of that house. There was work enough for him here; a kind voice told him so, a kind hand was laid on his shoulder, and he was bidden come and welcome. The tears rushed into the poor fellow's eyes, he went hastily away, and that night sent over his chest of tools,— he was a carpenter by trade. Next day he took up his abode here and worked all summer. Every day I carefully observed him as I passed him by, regarding him with an inexpressible pity, of which he was perfectly unconscious, as he seemed to be of everything and everybody. He never raised his head when he answered my "Good morning," or "Good evening, Ivan." Though I often wished to speak, I never said more to him, for he seemed to me to be hurt too sorely to be touched by human hand. With his head sunk on his breast, and wearily dragging his limbs, he pushed the plane or drove the saw to and fro with a kind of dogged persistence, looking neither to the left nor right. Well might the weight of woe he carried bow him to the earth! By and by he spoke, himself, to other members of the household, saying, with a patient sorrow, he believed it was to have been, it had been so ordered, else why did all things so play into Louis's hands? All things were furnished him: the knowledge of the unprotected state of the women, a perfectly clear field in which to carry out his plans, just the right boat he wanted in which to make his voyage, fair tide, fair wind, calm sea, just moonlight enough; even the ax with which to kill Anethe stood ready to his hand at the house door. Alas, it was to have been! Last summer Ivan went back again to Norway—alone. Hardly is it probable that he will ever return to a land whose welcome to him fate made so horrible. His sister Maren and her husband still live blameless lives, with the little dog Ringe, in a new home they have made for themselves in Portsmouth, not far from the river-side; the merciful lapse of days and years takes them gently but surely away from the thought of that season of anguish; and though they can never forget it all, they have grown resigned and quiet again. And on the island other Norwegians have settled, voices of charming children sound sweetly in the solitude that echoed so awfully to the shrieks of Karen and Maren. But to the weirdness of the winter midnight something is added, a vision of two dim, reproachful shades who watch while an agonized ghost prowls eternally about the dilapidated houses at the beach's edge, close by the black, whispering water, seeking for the woman who has escaped him—escaped to bring upon him the death he deserves, whom he never, never, never can find, though his distracted spirit may search till man shall vanish from off the face of the earth, and time shall be no more.

❧ | Ngaio Marsh

Ngaio Marsh, *who refers to herself as a spinster of uncertain years*, is the author of nearly two dozen of the best whodunits ever written. Miss Marsh is a New Zealander, and her unusual first name, rarely pronounced correctly (it should be ING-AH-EE-O), is the name of a New Zealand flower.

Miss Marsh wrote her first novel at the height of detective fever in England in 1932. It was one of those fortuitous accidents: she was sitting in a cold, dark, gloomy British room, with fog at the window and a detective story on the table. She read it, sat back, and decided she could write a better one, which led to a career that she has continued with great success. She says that her own ideas for "dark doings" come most successfully when she is vacuum cleaning.

Miss Marsh also says that the most gratifying compliment she ever received was from Sir Harold Scott, who was once the chief of Scotland Yard. That grand man of true detection said that he had read all her books and she had yet to "put a foot wrong."

Miss Marsh has a detective, Inspector Roderick Alleyn, who appears regularly in her books. As an author she depends heavily on unusual backgrounds and the new treatment of old themes. Perhaps because she was also an actress, many of her books have a theatrical background. In this early story she did not neglect what was then the omnipresent form of entertainment, radio.

The grand hands of detection have tried to work with unique subjects and unique settings. There are stories on almost every phase of contemporary life. Under the ABC's of murder, you can locate stories on advertising, amnesia, antiques, arson, artists, atomic research, ballet, bees, blackmail, children, Christmas. This story is about one family's Christmas Eve.

Death on the Air

On the 25th of December at 7:30 a.m. Mr. Septimus Tonks was found dead beside his wireless set.

It was Emily Parks, an under-housemaid, who discovered him. She butted open the door and entered, carrying mop, duster, and carpet-sweeper. At that precise moment she was greatly startled by a voice that spoke out of the darkness.

"Good morning, everybody," said the voice in superbly inflected syllables, "and a Merry Christmas!"

Emily yelped, but not loudly, as she immediately realized what had happened. Mr. Tonks had omitted to turn off his wireless before going to bed. She drew back the curtains, revealing a kind of pale murk which was a London Christmas dawn, switched on the light, and saw Septimus.

He was seated in front of the radio. It was a small but expensive set, specially built for him. Septimus sat in an armchair, his back to Emily, his body tilted towards the radio.

His hands, the fingers curiously bunched, were on the ledge of the cabinet under the tuning and volume knobs. His chest rested against the shelf below and his head leaned on the front panel.

He looked rather as though he was listening intently to the interior secrets of the wireless. His head was bent so that Emily could see his bald top with its trail of oiled hairs. He did not move.

"Beg pardon, sir," gasped Emily. She was again greatly

startled. Mr. Tonks' enthusiasm for radio had never before induced him to tune in at seven-thirty in the morning.

"Special Christmas service," the cultured voice was saying. Mr. Tonks sat very still. Emily, in common with the other servants, was terrified of her master. She did not know whether to go or to stay. She gazed wildly at Septimus and realized that he wore a dinner-jacket. The room was now filled with the clamor of pealing bells.

Emily opened her mouth as wide as it would go and screamed and screamed and screamed. . . .

Chase, the butler, was the first to arrive. He was a pale, flabby man but authoritative. He said: "What's the meaning of this outrage?" and then saw Septimus. He went to the arm-chair, bent down, and looked into his master's face.

He did not lose his head, but said in a loud voice: "My Gawd!" And then to Emily: "Shut your face." By this vulgarism he betrayed his agitation. He seized Emily by the shoulders and thrust her towards the door, where they were met by Mr. Hislop, the secretary, in his dressing-gown. Mr. Hislop said: "Good heavens, Chase, what is the meaning—" and then his voice too was drowned in the clamor of bells and renewed screams.

Chase put his fat white hand over Emily's mouth.

"In the study if you please, sir. An accident. Go to your room, will you, and stop that noise or I'll give you something to make you." This to Emily, who bolted down the hall, where she was received by the rest of the staff who had congregated there.

Chase returned to the study with Mr. Hislop and locked the door. They both looked down at the body of Septimus Tonks. The secretary was the first to speak.

"But—but—he's dead," said little Mr. Hislop.

"I suppose there can't be any doubt," whispered Chase.

"Look at the face. Any doubt! My God!"

Mr. Hislop put out a delicate hand towards the bent head and then drew it back. Chase, less fastidious, touched one of the hard wrists, gripped, and then lifted it. The body at once tipped backwards as if it was made of wood. One of the hands knocked against the butler's face. He sprang back with an oath.

There lay Septimus, his knees and his hands in the air, his terrible face turned up to the light. Chase pointed to the right hand. Two fingers and the thumb were slightly blackened.

Ding, dong, dang, ding.

"For God's sake stop those bells," cried Mr. Hislop. Chase turned off the wall switch. Into the sudden silence came the sound of the door-handle being rattled and Guy Tonks' voice on the other side.

"Hislop! Mr. Hislop! Chase! What's the matter?"

"Just a moment, Mr. Guy." Chase looked at the secretary. "You go, sir."

So it was left to Mr. Hislop to break the news to the family. They listened to his stammering revelation in stupefied silence. It was not until Guy, the eldest of the three children, stood in the study that any practical suggestion was made.

"What has killed him?" asked Guy.

"It's extraordinary," burbled Hislop. "Extraordinary. He looks as if he'd been—"

"Galvanized," said Guy.

"We ought to send for a doctor," suggested Hislop timidly.

"Of course. Will you, Mr. Hislop? Dr. Meadows."

Hislop went to the telephone and Guy returned to his family. Dr. Meadows lived on the other side of the square and arrived in five minutes. He examined the body without moving it. He questioned Chase and Hislop. Chase was very voluble about the burns on the hand. He uttered the word "electrocution" over and over again.

"I had a cousin, sir, that was struck by lightning. As soon as I saw the hand—"

"Yes, yes," said Dr. Meadows. "So you said. I can see the burns for myself."

"Electrocution," repeated Chase. "There'll have to be an inquest."

Dr. Meadows snapped at him, summoned Emily, and then saw the rest of the family—Guy, Arthur, Phillipa, and their mother. They were clustered round a cold grate in the drawing-room. Phillipa was on her knees, trying to light the fire.

"What was it?" asked Arthur as soon as the doctor came in.

"Looks like electric shock. Guy, I'll have a word with you if you please. Phillipa, look after your mother, there's a good child. Coffee with a dash of brandy. Where are those damn maids? Come on, Guy."

Alone with Guy, he said they'd have to send for the police.

"The police!" Guy's dark face turned very pale. "Why? What's it got to do with them?"

"Nothing, as like as not, but they'll have to be notified. I can't give a certificate as things are. If it's electrocution, how did it happen?"

"But the police!" said Guy. "That's simply ghastly. Dr. Meadows, for God's sake couldn't you—?"

"No," said Dr. Meadows, "I couldn't. Sorry, Guy, but there it is."

"But can't we wait a moment? Look at him again. You haven't examined him properly."

"I don't want to move him, that's why. Pull yourself together, boy. Look here. I've got a pal in the C.I.D.—Alleyn. He's a gentleman and all that. He'll curse me like a fury, but he'll come if he's in London, and he'll make things easier for you. Go back to your mother. I'll ring Alleyn up."

That was how it came about that Chief Detective-Inspector Roderick Alleyn spent his Christmas Day in harness. As a matter of fact he was on duty, and as he pointed out to Dr. Meadows, would have had to turn out and visit his miserable Tonkses in any case. When he did arrive it was with his usual air of remote courtesy. He was accompanied by a tall, thick-set officer—Inspector Fox—and by the divisional police-surgeon. Dr. Meadows took them into the study. Alleyn, in his turn, looked at the horror that had been Septimus.

"Was he like this when he was found?"

"No. I understand he was leaning forward with his hands on the ledge of the cabinet. He must have slumped forward and been propped up by the chair arms and the cabinet."

"Who moved him?"

"Chase, the butler. He said he only meant to raise the arm. *Rigor* is well established."

Alleyn put his hand behind the rigid neck and pushed. The body fell forward into its original position.

"There you are, Curtis," said Alleyn to the divisional surgeon. He turned to Fox. "Get the camera man, will you, Fox?"

The photographer took four shots and departed. Alleyn marked the position of the hands and feet with chalk, made a careful plan of the room and turned to the doctors.

"Is it electrocution, do you think?"

"Looks like it," said Curtis. "Have to be a p.m. of course."

"Of course. Still, look at the hands. Burns. Thumb and two fingers bunched together and exactly the distance between the two knobs apart. He'd been tuning his hurdy-gurdy."

"By gum," said Inspector Fox, speaking for the first time.

"D'you mean he got a lethal shock from his radio?" asked Dr. Meadows.

"I don't know. I merely conclude he had his hands on the knobs when he died."

"It was still going when the house-maid found him. Chase turned it off and got no shock."

"Yours, partner," said Alleyn, turning to Fox. Fox stooped down to the wall switch.

"Careful," said Alleyn.

"I've got rubber soles," said Fox, and switched it on. The radio hummed, gathered volume, and found itself.

"No-oel, No-o-el," it roared. Fox cut it off and pulled out the wall plug.

"I'd like to have a look inside this set," he said.

"So you shall, old boy, so you shall," rejoined Alleyn. "Before you begin, I think we'd better move the body. Will you see to that, Meadows? Fox, get Bailey, will you? He's out in the car."

Curtis, Hislop, and Meadows carried Septimus Tonks into a spare downstairs room. It was a difficult and horrible business with that contorted body. Dr. Meadows came back alone, mopping his brow, to find Detective-Sergeant Bailey, a fingerprint expert, at work on the wireless cabinet.

"What's all this?" asked Dr. Meadows. "Do you want to find out if he'd been fooling round with the innards?"

"He," said Alleyn, "or—somebody else."

"Umph!" Dr. Meadows looked at the Inspector. "You agree with me, it seems. Do you suspect—?"

"Suspect? I'm the least suspicious man alive. I'm merely being tidy. Well, Bailey?"

"I've got a good one off the chair arm. That'll be the deceased's, won't it, sir?"

"No doubt. We'll check up later. What about the wireless?"

Fox, wearing a glove, pulled off the knob of the volume control.

"Seems to be O.K." said Bailey. "It's a sweet bit of work. Not too bad at all, sir." He turned his torch into the back of the radio, undid a couple of screws underneath the set, lifted out the works.

"What's the little hole for?" asked Alleyn.

"What's that, sir?" said Fox.

"There's a hole-bored through the panel above the knob. About an eighth of an inch in diameter. The rim of the knob hides it. One might easily miss it. Move your torch, Bailey. Yes. There, do you see?"

Fox bent down and uttered a bass growl. A fine needle of light came through the front of the radio.

"That's peculiar, sir," said Bailey from the other side. "I don't get the idea at all."

Alleyn pulled out the tuning knob.

"There's another one there," he murmured. "Yes. Nice clean little holes. Newly bored. Unusual, I take it?"

"Unusual's the word, sir," said Fox.

"Run away, Meadows," said Alleyn.

"Why the devil?" asked Dr. Meadows indignantly. "What are you driving at? Why shouldn't I be here?"

"You ought to be with the sorrowing relatives. Where's your corpseside manner?"

"I've settled them. What are you up to?"

"Who's being suspicious now?" asked Alleyn mildly. "You may stay for a moment. Tell me about the Tonkses. Who are they? What are they? What sort of a man was Septimus?"

"If you must know, he was a damned unpleasant sort of a man."

"Tell me about him."

Dr. Meadows sat down and lit a cigarette.

"He was a self-made bloke," he said, "as hard as nails and—well, coarse rather than vulgar."

"Like Dr. Johnson perhaps?"

"Not in the least. Don't interrupt. I've known him for twenty-five years. His wife was a neighbor of ours in Dorset. Isabel Foreston. I brought the children into this vale of tears and, by jove, in many ways it's been one for them. It's an extraordinary household. For the last ten years Isabel's condition has been the sort that sends these psycho-jokers dizzy with rapture. I'm only an out-of-date G.P., and I'd just say she is in an advanced stage of hysterical neurosis. Frightened into fits of her husband."

"I can't understand these holes," grumbled Fox to Bailey.

"Go on, Meadows," said Alleyn.

"I tackled Sep about her eighteen months ago. Told him the trouble was in her mind. He eyed me with a sort of grin on his face and said: 'I'm surprised to learn that my wife has enough mentality to—' But look here, Alleyn, I can't talk about my patients like this. What the devil am I thinking about."

"You know perfectly well it'll go no further unless—"

"Unless what?"

"Unless it has to. Do go on."

But Dr. Meadows hurriedly withdrew behind his professional rectitude. All he would say was that Mr. Tonks had suffered from high blood pressure and a weak heart, that Guy was in his father's city office, that Arthur had wanted to study art and had been told to read for law, and that Phillipa wanted to go on the stage and had been told to do nothing of the sort.

"Bullied his children," commented Alleyn.

"Find out for yourself. I'm off." Dr. Meadows got as far as the door and came back.

"Look here," he said, "I'll tell you one thing. There was a row here last night. I'd asked Hislop, who's a sensible little beggar, to let me know if anything happened to upset Mrs. Sep. Upset her badly, you know. To be indiscreet again, I said he'd better let me know if Sep cut up rough because Isabel and the young had had about as much of that as they could stand. He was drinking pretty heavily. Hislop rang me up at ten-twenty last night to say there'd been a hell of a row; Sep bullying Phips —Phillipa, you know; always call her Phips—in her room. He said Isabel—Mrs. Sep—had gone to bed. I'd had a big day and I didn't want to turn out. I told him to ring again in half an hour if things hadn't quieted down. I told him to keep out of Sep's way and stay in his own room, which is next to Phips' and see if she was all right when Sep cleared out. Hislop was involved. I won't tell you how. The servants were all out. I said that if I didn't hear from him in half an hour I'd ring again and if there was no answer I'd know they were all in bed and quiet. I did ring, got no answer, and went to bed myself. That's all. I'm off. Curtis knows where to find me. You'll want me for the inquest, I suppose. Goodbye."

When he had gone Alleyn embarked on a systematic prowl round the room. Fox and Bailey were still deeply engrossed with the wireless.

"I don't see how the gentleman could have got a bump-off from the instrument," grumbled Fox. "These control knobs are quite in order. Everything's as it should be. Look here, sir."

He turned on the wall switch and tuned in. There was a prolonged humming.

". . . concludes the program of Christmas carols," said the radio.

"A very nice tone," said Fox approvingly.

"Here's something, sir," announced Bailey suddenly.

"Found the sawdust, have you?" said Alleyn.

"Got it in one," said the startled Bailey.

Alleyn peered into the instrument, using the torch. He scooped up two tiny traces of sawdust from under the holes.

" 'Vantage number one," said Alleyn. He bent down to the wall plug. "Hullo! A two-way adapter. Serves the radio and the radiator. Thought they were illegal. This is a rum business. Let's have another look at those knobs."

He had his look. They were the usual wireless fitments, bakelite knobs fitting snugly to the steel shafts that projected from the front panel.

"As you say," he murmured, "quite in order. Wait a bit." He produced a pocket lens and squinted at one of the shafts. "Ye-es.

Do they ever wrap blotting-paper round these objects, Fox?"

"Blotting-paper!" ejaculated Fox. "They do not."

Alleyn scraped at both the shafts with his penknife, holding an envelope underneath. He rose, groaning, and crossed to the desk. "A corner torn off the bottom bit of blotch," he said presently. "No prints on the wireless, I think you said, Bailey?"

"That's right," agreed Bailey morosely.

"There'll be none, or too many, on the blotter, but try, Bailey, try," said Alleyn. He wandered about the room, his eyes on the floor; got as far as the window and stopped.

"Fox!" he said. "A clue. A very palpable clue."

"What is it?" asked Fox.

"The odd wisp of blotting-paper, no less." Alleyn's gaze traveled up the side of the window curtain. "Can I believe my eyes?"

He got a chair, stood on the seat, and with his gloved hand pulled the buttons from the ends of the curtain rod.

"Look at this." He turned to the radio, detached the control knobs, and laid them beside the ones he had removed from the curtain rod.

Ten minutes later Inspector Fox knocked on the drawing-room door and was admitted by Guy Tonks. Phillipa had got the fire going and the family was gathered round it. They looked as though they had not moved or spoken to one another for a long time.

It was Phillipa who spoke first to Fox. "Do you want one of us?"

"If you please, miss," said Fox. "Inspector Alleyn would like to see Mr. Guy Tonks for a moment, if convenient."

"I'll come," said Guy, and led the way to the study. At the door he paused. "Is he—my father—still—?"

"No, no, sir," said Fox comfortably. "It's all ship-shape in there again."

With a lift of his chin Guy opened the door and went in, followed by Fox. Alleyn was alone, seated at the desk. He rose to his feet.

"You want to speak to me?" asked Guy.

"Yes, if I may. This has all been a great shock to you, of course. Won't you sit down?"

Guy sat in the chair farthest away from the radio.

"What killed my father? Was it a stroke?"

"The doctors are not quite certain. There will have to be a *post-mortem*."

"Good God! And an inquest?"

"I'm afraid so."

"Horrible!" said Guy violently. "What do you think was the matter? Why the devil do these quacks have to be so mysterious? What killed him?"

"They think an electric shock."

"How did it happen?"

"We don't know. It looks as if he got it from the wireless."

"Surely that's impossible. I thought they were fool-proof."

"I believe they are, if left to themselves."

For a second undoubtedly Guy was startled. Then a look of relief came into his eyes. He seemed to relax all over.

"Of course," he said, "he was always monkeying about with it. What had he done?"

"Nothing."

"But you said—if it killed him he must have done something to it."

"If anyone interfered with the set it was put right afterwards."

Guy's lips parted but he did not speak. He had gone very white.

"So you see," said Alleyn, "your father could not have done anything."

"Then it was not the radio that killed him."

"That we hope will be determined by the *post-mortem*."

"I don't know anything about wireless," said Guy suddenly. "I don't understand. This doesn't seem to make sense. Nobody ever touched the thing except my father. He was most particular about it. Nobody went near the wireless."

"I see. He was an enthusiast?"

"Yes, it was his only enthusiasm except—except his business."

"One of my men is a bit of an expert," Alleyn said. "He says this is a remarkably good set. You are not an expert you say. Is there anyone in the house who is?"

"My young brother was interested at one time. He's given it up. My father wouldn't allow another radio in the house."

"Perhaps he may be able to suggest something."

"But if the thing's all right now—"

"We've got to explore every possibility."

"You speak as if—as—if—"

"I speak as I am bound to speak before there has been an inquest," said Alleyn. "Had anyone a grudge against your father, Mr. Tonks?"

Up went Guy's chin again. He looked Alleyn squarely in the eyes.

"Almost everyone who knew him," said Guy.

"Is that an exaggeration?"

"No. You think he was murdered, don't you?"

Alleyn suddenly pointed to the desk beside him.

"Have you ever seen those before?" he asked abruptly. Guy stared at two black knobs that lay side by side on an ashtray.

"Those?" he said. "No. What are they?"

"I believe they are the agents of your father's death."

The study door opened and Arthur Tonks came in.

"Guy," he said, "what's happening? We can't stay cooped up together all day. I can't stand it. For God's sake what happened to him?"

"They think those things killed him," said Guy.

"Those?" For a split second Arthur's glance slewed to the

curtainrods. Then, with a characteristic flicker of his eyelids, he looked away again.

"What do you mean?" he asked Alleyn.

"Will you try one of those knobs on the shaft of the volume control?"

"But," said Arthur, "they're metal."

"It's disconnected," said Alleyn.

Arthur picked one of the knobs from the tray, turned to the radio, and fitted the knob over one of the exposed shafts.

"It's too loose," he said quickly, "it would fall off."

"Not if it was packed—with blotting-paper, for instance."

"Where did you find these things?" demanded Arthur.

"I think you recognized them, didn't you? I saw you glance at the curtain-rod."

"Of course I recognized them. I did a portrait of Phillipa against those curtains when—he—was away last year. I've painted the damn things."

"Look here," interrupted Guy, "exactly what are you driving at, Mr. Alleyn? If you mean to suggest that my brother—"

"I!" cried Arthur. "What's it got to do with me? Why should you suppose—."

"I found traces of blotting-paper on the shafts and inside the metal knobs," said Alleyn. "It suggested a substitution of the metal knobs for the bakelite ones. It is remarkable, don't you think, that they should so closely resemble one another? If you examine them, of course, you find they are not identical. Still, the difference is scarcely perceptible."

Arthur did not answer this. He was still looking at the wireless.

"I've always wanted to have a look at this set," he said surprisingly.

"You are free to do so now," said Alleyn politely. "We have finished with it for the time being."

"Look here," said Arthur suddenly, "suppose metal knobs

were substituted for bakelite ones, it couldn't kill him. He wouldn't get a shock at all. Both the controls are grounded."

"Have you noticed those very small holes drilled through the panel?" asked Alleyn. "Should they be there, do you think?"

Arthur peered at the little steel shafts. "By God, he's right, Guy," he said. "That's how it was done."

"Inspector Fox," said Alleyn, "tells me those holes could be used for conducting wires and that a lead could be taken from the—the transformer, is it?—to one of the knobs."

"And the other connected to earth," said Fox. "It's a job for an expert. He could get three hundred volts or so that way."

"That's not good enough," said Arthur quickly; "there wouldn't be enough current to do any damage—only a few hundredths of an amp."

"I'm not an expert," said Alleyn, "but I'm sure you're right. Why were the holes drilled then? Do you imagine someone wanted to play a practical joke on your father?"

"A practical joke? On *him*?" Arthur gave an unpleasant screech of laughter. "Do you hear that, Guy?"

"Shut up," said Guy. "After all, he is dead."

"It seems almost too good to be true, doesn't it?"

"Don't be a bloody fool, Arthur. Pull yourself together. Can't you see what this means? They think he's been murdered."

"Murdered! They're wrong. None of us had the nerve for that, Mr. Inspector. Look at me. My hands are so shaky they told me I'd never be able to paint. That dates from when I was a kid and he shut me up in the cellars for a night. Look at me. Look at Guy. He's not so vulnerable, but he caved in like the rest of us. We were conditioned to surrender. Do you know—"

"Wait a moment," said Alleyn quietly. "Your brother is quite right, you know. You'd better think before you speak. This may be a case of homicide."

"Thank you, sir," said Guy quickly. "That's extraordinarily

decent of you. Arthur's a bit above himself. It's a shock."

"The relief, you mean," said Arthur. "Don't be such an ass. I didn't kill him and they'll find it out soon enough. Nobody killed him. There must be some explanation."

"I suggest that you listen to me," said Alleyn. "I'm going to put several questions to both of you. You need not answer them, but it will be more sensible to do so. I understand no one but your father touched this radio. Did any of you ever come into this room while it was in use?"

"Not unless he wanted to vary the program with a little bullying," said Arthur.

Alleyn turned to Guy, who was glaring at his brother.

"I want to know exactly what happened in this house last night. As far as the doctors can tell us, your father died not less than three and not more than eight hours before he was found. We must try to fix the time as accurately as possible."

"I saw him at about a quarter to nine," began Guy slowly. "I was going out to a supper-party at the Savoy and had come downstairs. He was crossing the hall from the drawing-room to his room."

"Did you see him after a quarter to nine, Mr. Arthur?"

"No. I heard him, though. He was working in here with Hislop. Hislop had asked to go away for Christmas. Quite enough. My father discovered some urgent correspondence. Really, Guy, you know, he was pathological. I'm sure Dr. Meadows thinks so."

"When did you hear him?" asked Alleyn.

"Some time after Guy had gone. I was working on a drawing in my room upstairs. It's above his. I heard him bawling at little Hislop. It must have been before ten o'clock, because I went out to a studio party at ten. I heard him bawling as I crossed the hall."

"And when," said Alleyn, "did you both return?"

"I came home at about twenty past twelve," said Guy immediately. "I can fix the time because we had gone on to Chez Carlo, and they had a midnight stunt there. We left immediately afterwards. I came home in a taxi. The radio was on full blast."

"You heard no voices?"

"None. Just the wireless."

"And you, Mr. Arthur?"

"Lord knows when I got in. After one. The house was in darkness. Not a sound."

"You had your own key?"

"Yes," said Guy. "Each of us has one. They're always left on a hook in the lobby. When I came in I noticed Arthur's was gone."

"What about the others? How did you know it was his?"

"Mother hasn't got one and Phips lost hers weeks ago. Anyway, I knew they were staying in and that it must be Arthur who was out."

"Thank you," said Arthur ironically.

"You didn't look in the study when you came in," Alleyn asked him.

"Good Lord, no," said Arthur as if the suggestion was fantastic. "I say," he said suddenly, "I suppose he was sitting here—dead. That's a queer thought." He laughed nervously. "Just sitting here, behind the door in the dark."

"How do you know it was in the dark?"

"What d'you mean? Of course it was. There was no light under the door."

"I see. Now do you two mind joining your mother again? Perhaps your sister will be kind enough to come in here for a moment. Fox, ask her, will you?"

Fox returned to the drawing-room with Guy and Arthur and remained there, blandly unconscious of any embarrassment his presence might cause the Tonkses. Bailey was already there, ostensibly examining the electric points.

Phillipa went to the study at once. Her first remark was characteristic. "Can I be of any help?" asked Phillipa.

"It's extremely nice of you to put it like that," said Alleyn. "I don't want to worry you for long. I'm sure this discovery has been a shock to you."

"Probably," said Phillipa. Alleyn glanced quickly at her. "I mean," she explained, "that I suppose I must be shocked but I can't feel anything much. I just want to get it all over as soon as possible. And then think. Please tell me what has happened."

Alleyn told her they believed her father had been electrocuted and that the circumstances were unusual and puzzling. He said nothing to suggest that the police suspected murder.

"I don't think I'll be much help," said Phillipa, "but go ahead."

"I want to try to discover who was the last person to see your father or speak to him."

"I should think very likely I was," said Phillipa composedly. "I had a row with him before I went to bed."

"What about?"

"I don't see that it matters."

Alleyn considered this. When he spoke again it was with deliberation.

"Look here," he said, "I think there is very little doubt that your father was killed by an electric shock from his wireless set. As far as I know the circumstances are unique. Radios are normally incapable of giving a lethal shock to anyone. We have examined the cabinet and are inclined to think that its internal arrangements were disturbed last night. Very radically disturbed. Your father may have experimented with it. If anything happened to interrupt or upset him, it is possible that in the excitement of the moment he made some dangerous readjustment."

"You don't believe that, do you?" asked Phillipa calmly.

"Since you ask me," said Alleyn, "no."

"I see," said Phillipa; "you think he was murdered, but you're not sure." She had gone very white, but she spoke crisply. "Naturally you want to find out about my row."

"About everything that happened last evening," amended Alleyn.

"What happened was this," said Phillipa; "I came into the hall some time after ten. I'd heard Arthur go out and had looked at the clock at five past. I ran into my father's secretary, Richard Hislop. He turned aside, but not before I saw . . . not quickly enough. I blurted out: 'You're crying.' We looked at each other. I asked him why he stood it. None of the other secretaries could. He said he had to. He's a widower with two children. There have been doctor's bills and things. I needn't tell you about his . . . about his damnable servitude to my father nor about the refinements of cruelty he'd had to put up with. I think my father was mad, really mad, I mean. Richard gabbled it all out to me higgledy-piggledy in a sort of horrified whisper. He's been here two years, but I'd never realized until that moment that we . . . that . . ." A faint flush came into her cheeks. "He's such a funny little man. Not at all the sort I've always thought . . . not good-looking or exciting or anything."

She stopped, looking bewildered.

"Yes?" said Alleyn.

"Well, you see—I suddenly realized I was in love with him. He realized it too. He said: 'Of course, it's quite hopeless, you know. Us, I mean. Laughable, almost.' Then I put my arms round his neck and kissed him. It was very odd, but it seemed quite natural. The point is my father came out of his room into the hall and saw us."

"That was bad luck," said Alleyn.

"Yes, it was. My father really seemed delighted. He almost licked his lips. Richard's efficiency had irritated my father for a long time. It was difficult to find excuses for being beastly to him. Now, of course . . . He ordered Richard to the study and me to my room. He followed me upstairs. Richard tried to come too, but I asked him not to. My father . . . I needn't tell you what he said. He put the worst possible construction on what he'd seen. He was absolutely foul, screaming at me like a madman. He was insane. Perhaps it was D. Ts. He drank terribly, you know. I dare say it's silly of me to tell you all this."

"No," said Alleyn.

"I can't feel anything at all. Not even relief. The boys are frankly relieved. I can't feel afraid either." She stared meditatively at Alleyn. "Innocent people needn't feel afraid, need they?"

"It's an axiom of police investigation," said Alleyn and wondered if indeed she was innocent.

"It just *can't* be murder," said Phillipa. "We were all too much afraid to kill him. I believe he'd win even if you murdered him. He'd hit back somehow." She put her hands to her eyes. "I'm all muddled."

"I think you are more upset than you realize. I'll be as quick as I can. Your father made this scene in your room. You say he screamed. Did anyone hear him?"

"Yes. Mummy did. She came in."

"What happened?"

"I said: 'Go away, darling, it's all right.' I didn't want her to be involved. He nearly killed her with the things he did. Sometimes he'd . . . we never knew what happened between them. It was all secret, like a door shutting quietly as you walk along a passage."

"Did she go away?"

"Not at once. He told her he'd found out that Richard and I were lovers. He said . . . it doesn't matter. I don't want to tell you. She was terrified. He was stabbing at her in some way I couldn't understand. Then, quite suddenly, he told her to go to her own room. She went at once and he followed her. He locked me in. That's the last I saw of him, but I heard him go downstairs later."

"Were you locked in all night?"

"No. Richard Hislop's room is next to mine. He came up and spoke through the wall to me. He wanted to unlock the door, but I said better not in case—he—came back. Then, much later, Guy came home. As he passed my door I tapped on it. The key was in the lock and he turned it."

"Did you tell him what had happened?"

"Just that there'd been a row. He only stayed a moment."

"Can you hear the radio from your room?"

She seemed surprised.

"The wireless? Why, yes. Faintly."

"Did you hear it after your father returned to the study?"

"I don't remember."

"Think. While you lay awake all that long time until your brother came home?"

"I'll try. When he came out and found Richard and me, it was not going. They had been working, you see. No, I can't remember hearing it at all unless—wait a moment. Yes. After he had gone back to the study from mother's room I remember there was a loud crash of static. Very loud. Then I think it was quiet for some time. I fancy I heard it again later. Oh, I've remembered something else. After the static my bedside radiator went out. I suppose there was something wrong with the electric supply. That would account for both, wouldn't it? The heater went on again about ten minutes later."

"And did the radio begin again then, do you think?"

"I don't know. I'm very vague about that. It started again sometime before I went to sleep."

"Thank you very much indeed. I won't bother you any longer now."

"All right," said Phillipa calmly, and went away.

Alleyn sent for Chase and questioned him about the rest of the staff and about the discovery of the body. Emily was summoned and dealt with. When she departed, awestruck but complacent, Alleyn turned to the butler.

"Chase," he said, "had your master any peculiar habits?"

"Yes, sir."

"In regard to the wireless?"

"I beg pardon, sir. I thought you meant generally speaking."

"Well, then, generally speaking."

"If I may so, sir, he was a mass of them."

"How long have you been with him?"

"Two months, sir, and due to leave at the end of this week."

"Oh. Why are you leaving?"

Chase produced the classic remark of his kind.

"There are some things," he said, "that flesh and blood will not stand, sir. One of them's being spoke to like Mr. Tonks spoke to his staff."

"Ah. His peculiar habits, in fact?"

"It's my opinion, sir, he was mad. Stark, staring."

"With regard to the radio. Did he tinker with it?"

"I can't say I've ever noticed, sir. I believe he knew quite a lot about wireless."

"When he tuned the thing, had he any particular method? Any characteristic attitude or gesture?"

"I don't think so, sir. I never noticed, and yet I've often come into the room when he was at it. I can seem to see him now, sir."

"Yes, yes," said Alleyn swiftly. "That's what we want. A clear mental picture. How was it now? Like this?"

In a moment he was across the room and seated in Septimus's chair. He swung round to the cabinet and raised his right hand to the tuning control.

"Like this?"

"No, sir," said Chase promptly, "that's not him at all. Both hands it should be."

"Ah." Up went Alleyn's left hand to the volume control. "More like this?"

"Yes, sir," said Chase slowly. "But there's something else and I can't recollect what it was. Something he was always doing. It's in the back of my head. You know, sir. Just on the edge of my memory, as you might say."

"I know."

"It's a kind—something—to do with irritation," said Chase slowly.

"Irritation? His?"

"No. It's no good, sir. I can't get it."

"Perhaps later. Now look here, Chase, what happened to all of you last night? All the servants, I mean."

"We were all out, sir. It being Christmas Eve. The mistress sent for me yesterday morning. She said we could take the evening off as soon as I had taken in Mr. Tonks's grog-tray at nine o'clock. So we went," ended Chase simply.

"When?"

"The rest of the staff got away about nine. I left at ten past, sir, and returned about eleven-twenty. The others were back then, and all in bed. I went straight to bed myself, sir."

"You came in by a back door, I suppose?"

"Yes, sir. We've been talking it over. None of us noticed anything unusual."

"Can you hear the wireless in your part of the house?"

"No, sir."

"Well," said Alleyn, looking up from his notes, "that'll do, thank you."

Before Chase reached the door Fox came in.

"Beg pardon, sir," said Fox, "I just want to take a look at the *Radio Times* on the desk."

He bent over the paper, wetted a gigantic thumb, and turned a page.

"That's it, sir," shouted Chase suddenly. "That's what I tried to think of. That's what he was always doing."

"But what?"

"Licking his fingers, sir. It was a habit," said Chase. "That's what he always did when he sat down to the radio. I heard Mr. Hislop tell the doctor it nearly drove him demented, the way the master couldn't touch a thing without first licking his fingers."

"Quite so," said Alleyn. "In about ten minutes, ask Mr. Hislop if he will be good enough to come in for a moment. That will be all, thank you, Chase."

"Well, sir," remarked Fox when Chase had gone, "if that's the case and what I think's right, it'd certainly make matters worse."

"Good heavens, Fox, what an elaborate remark. What does it mean?"

"If metal knobs were substituted for bakelite ones and fine wires brought through those holes to make contact, then he'd get a bigger bump if he tuned in with *damp* fingers."

"Yes. And he always used both hands. Fox!"

"Sir."

"Approach the Tonkses again. You haven't left them alone, of course?"

"Bailey's in there making out he's interested in the light switches. He's found the main switchboard under the stairs. There's signs of a blown fuse having been fixed recently. In a cupboard underneath there are odd lengths of flex and so on. Same brand as this on the wireless and the heater."

"Ah, yes. Could the cord from the adapter to the radiator be brought into play?"

"By gum," said Fox, "you're right! That's how it was done,

Chief. The heavier flex was cut away from the radiator and shoved through. There was a fire, so he wouldn't want the radiator and wouldn't notice."

"It might have been done that way, certainly, but there's little to prove it. Return to the bereaved Tonkses, my Fox, and ask prettily if any of them remember Septimus's peculiarities when tuning his wireless."

Fox met little Mr. Hislop at the door and left him alone with Alleyn. Phillipa had been right, reflected the Inspector, when she said Richard Hislop was not a noticeable man. He was nondescript. Grey eyes, drab hair; rather pale, rather short, rather insignificant; and yet last night there had flashed up between those two the realization of love. Romantic but rum, thought Alleyn.

"Do sit down," he said. "I want you, if you will, to tell me what happened between you and Mr. Tonks last evening."

"What happened?"

"Yes. You all dined at eight, I understand. Then you and Mr. Tonks came in here?"

"Yes."

"What did you do?"

"He dictated several letters."

"Anything unusual take place?"

"Oh, no."

"Why did you quarrel?"

"Quarrel!" The quiet voice jumped a tone. "We did not quarrel, Mr. Alleyn."

"Perhaps that was the wrong word. What upset you?"

"Phillipa has told you?"

"Yes. She was wise to do so. What was the matter, Mr. Hislop?"

"Apart from the . . . what she told you . . . Mr. Tonks was a difficult man to please. I often irritated him. I did so last night."

"In what way?"

"In almost every way. He shouted at me. I was startled and nervous, clumsy with papers, and making mistakes. I wasn't well. I blundered and then . . . I . . . I broke down. I have always irritated him. My very mannerisms—"

"Had he no irritating mannerisms, himself?"

"He! My God!"

"What were they?"

"I can't think of anything in particular. It doesn't matter does it?"

"Anything to do with the wireless, for instance?"

There was a short silence.

"No," said Hislop.

"Was the radio on in here last night, after dinner?"

"For a little while. Not after—after the incident in the hall. At least, I don't think so. I don't remember."

"What did you do after Miss Phillipa and her father had gone upstairs?"

"I followed and listened outside the door for a moment." He had gone very white and had backed away from the desk.

"And then?"

"I heard someone coming. I remembered Dr. Meadows had told me to ring him up if there was one of the scenes. I returned here and rang him up. He told me to go to my room and listen. If things got any worse I was to telephone again. Otherwise I was to stay in my room. It is next to hers."

"And you did this?" He nodded. "Could you hear what Mr. Tonks said to her?"

"A—a good deal of it."

"What did you hear?"

"He insulted her. Mrs. Tonks was there. I was just thinking of ringing Dr. Meadows up again when she and Mr. Tonks came out and went along the passage. I stayed in my room."

"You did not try to speak to Miss Phillipa?"

"We spoke through the wall. She asked me not to ring Dr. Meadows, but to stay in my room. In a little while, perhaps it was as much as twenty minutes—I really don't know—I heard him come back and go downstairs. I again spoke to Phillipa. She implored me not to do anything and said that she herself would speak to Dr. Meadows in the morning. So I waited a little longer and then went to bed."

"And to sleep?"

"My God, no!"

"Did you hear the wireless again?"

"Yes. At least I heard static."

"Are you an expert on wireless?"

"No. I know the ordinary things. Nothing much."

"How did you come to take this job, Mr. Hislop?"

"I answered an advertisement."

"You are sure you don't remember any particular mannerism of Mr. Tonks's in connection with the radio?"

"No."

"And you can tell me no more about your interview in the study that led to the scene in the hall?"

"No."

"Will you please ask Mrs. Tonks if she will be kind enough to speak to me for a moment?"

"Certainly," said Hislop, and went away.

Septimus's wife came in looking like death. Alleyn got her to sit down and asked her about her movements on the preceding evening. She said she was feeling unwell and dined in her room. She went to bed immediately afterwards. She heard Septimus yelling at Phillipa and went to Phillipa's room. Septimus accused Mr. Hislop and her daughter of "terrible things." She got as far as this and then broke down quietly. Alleyn was very gentle with her. After a little while he learned that Septimus had gone to her room with her and had continued to speak of "terrible things."

"What sort of things?" asked Alleyn.

"He was not responsible," said Isabel. "He did not know what he was saying. I think he had been drinking."

She thought he had remained with her for perhaps a quarter of an hour. Possibly longer. He left her abruptly and she heard him go along the passage, past Phillipa's door, and presumably downstairs. She had stayed awake for a long time. The wireless could not be heard from her room. Alleyn showed her the curtain knobs, but she seemed quite unable to take in their significance. He let her go, summoned Fox, and went over the whole case.

"What's your idea on the show?" he asked when he had finished.

"Well, sir," said Fox, in his stolid way, "on the face of it the young gentlemen have got alibis. We'll have to check them up, of course, and I don't see we can go much further until we have done so."

"For the moment," said Alleyn, "let us suppose Masters Guy and Arthur to be safely established behind cast-iron alibis. What then?"

"Then we've got the young lady, the old lady, the secretary, and the servants."

"Let us parade them. But first let us go over the wireless game. You'll have to watch me here. I gather that the only way in which the radio could be fixed to give Mr. Tonks his quietus is like this: Control knobs removed. Holes bored in front panel with fine drill. Metal knobs substituted and packed with blotting paper to insulate them from metal shafts and make them stay put. Heavier flex from adapter to radiator cut and the ends of the wires pushed through the drilled holes to make contact with the new knobs. Thus we have a positive and negative pole. Mr. Tonks bridges the gap, gets a mighty wallop as the current passes through him to the earth. The switchboard fuse is blown almost immediately. All this is rigged by murderer while Sep was upstairs bullying wife and daughter. Sep revisited study some time after ten-twenty. Whole thing was made ready between ten, when Arthur went out, and the time Sep returned—say, about ten-forty-five. The murderer reappeared, connected radiator with flex, removed wires, changed back knobs, and left the thing tuned in. Now I take it that the burst of static described by Phillipa and Hislop would be caused by the short-circuit that killed our Septimus?"

"That's right."

"It also affected all the heaters in the house. *Vide* Miss Tonks's radiator."

"Yes. He put all that right again. It would be a simple enough matter for anyone who knew how. He'd just have to fix the fuse on the main switchboard. How long do you say it would take to—what's the horrible word?—to recondition the whole show?"

"M'm," said Fox deeply. "At a guess, sir, fifteen minutes. He'd have to be nippy."

"Yes," agreed Alleyn. "He or she."

"I don't see a female making a success of it," grunted Fox. "Look here, Chief, you know what I'm thinking. Why did Mr. Hislop lie about deceased's habit of licking his thumbs? You say Hislop told you he remembered nothing and Chase says he overheard him saying the trick nearly drove him dippy."

"Exactly," said Alleyn. He was silent for so long that Fox felt moved to utter a discreet cough.

"Eh?" said Alleyn. "Yes, Fox, yes. It'll have to be done." He consulted the telephone directory and dialed a number.

"May I speak to Dr. Meadows? Oh, it's you, is it? Do you remember Mr. Hislop telling you that Septimus Tonks's trick of wetting his fingers nearly drove Hislop demented. Are you there? You don't? Sure? All right. All right. Hislop rang you up at ten-twenty, you said? And you telephoned him? At eleven. Sure of the times? I see. I'd be glad if you'd come round. Can you? Well, do if you can."

He hung up the receiver.

"Get Chase again, will you, Fox?"

Chase, recalled, was most insistent that Mr. Hislop had spoken about it to Dr. Meadows.

"It was when Mr. Hislop had flu, sir. I went up with the doctor. Mr. Hislop had a high temperature and was talking very excited. He kept on and on, saying the master had guessed his ways had driven him crazy and that the master kept on purposely to aggravate. He said if it went on much longer he'd . . . he didn't know what he was talking about, sir, really."

"What did he say he'd do?"

"Well, sir, he said he'd—he'd do something desperate to the master. But it was only his rambling, sir. I daresay he wouldn't remember anything about it."

"No," said Alleyn, "I daresay he wouldn't." When Chase had gone he said to Fox: "Go and find out about those boys and their alibis. See if they can put you on to a quick means of checking up. Get Master Guy to corroborate Miss Phillipa's statement that she was locked in her room."

Fox had been gone for some time and Alleyn was still busy with his notes when the study door burst open and in came Dr. Meadows.

"Look here, my giddy sleuth-hound," he shouted, "what's all this about Hislop? Who says he disliked Sep's abominable habits?"

"Chase does. And don't bawl at me like that. I'm worried."

"So am I, blast you. What are you driving at? You can't imagine that . . . that poor little broken-down hack is capable of electrocuting anybody, let alone Sep?"

"I have no imagination," said Alleyn wearily.

"I wish to God I hadn't called you in. If the wireless killed Sep, it was because he'd monkeyed with it."

"And put it right after it had killed him?"

Dr. Meadows stared at Alleyn in silence.

"Now," said Alleyn, "you've got to give me a straight answer, Meadows. Did Hislop, while he was semi-delirious, say that this habit of Tonks's made him feel like murdering him?"

"I'd forgotten Chase was there," said Dr. Meadows.

"Yes, you'd forgotten that."

"But even if he did talk wildly, Alleyn, what of it? Damn it, you can't arrest a man on the strength of a remark made in delirium."

"I don't propose to do so. Another motive has come to light."

"You mean—Phips—last night?"

"Did he tell you about that?"

"She whispered something to me this morning. I'm very fond of Phips. My God, are you sure of your grounds?"

"Yes," said Alleyn. "I'm sorry. I think you'd better go, Meadows."

"Are you going to arrest him?"

"I have to do my job."

There was a long silence.

"Yes," said Dr. Meadows at last. "You have to do your job. Goodbye, Alleyn."

Fox returned to say that Guy and Arthur had never left their parties. He had got hold of two of their friends. Guy and Mrs. Tonks confirmed the story of the locked door.

"It's a process of elimination," said Fox. "It must be the secretary. He fixed the radio while deceased was upstairs. He must have dodged back to whisper through the door to Miss Tonks. I suppose he waited somewhere down here until he heard deceased blow himself to blazes and then put everything straight again, leaving the radio turned on."

Alleyn was silent.

"What do we do now, sir?" asked Fox.

"I want to see the hook inside the front-door where they hang their keys."

Fox, looking dazed, followed his superior to the little entrance hall.

"Yes, there they are," said Alleyn. He pointed to a hook with two latch-keys hanging from it. "You could scarcely miss them. Come on, Fox."

Back in the study they found Hislop with Bailey in attendance.

Hislop looked from one Yard man to another.

"I want to know if it's murder."

"We think so," said Alleyn.

"I want you to realize that Phillipa—Miss Tonks—was locked in her room all last night."

"Until her brother came home and unlocked the door," said Alleyn.

"That was too late. He was dead by then."

"How do you know when he died?"

"It must have been when there was that crash of static."

"Mr. Hislop," said Alleyn, "why would you not tell me how much that trick of licking his fingers exasperated you?"

"But—how do you know! I never told anyone."

"You told Dr. Meadows when you were ill."

"I don't remember." He stopped short. His lips trembled. Then, suddenly he began to speak.

"Very well. It's true. For two years he's tortured me. You see, he knew something about me. Two years ago when my wife was dying, I took money from the cash-box in that desk. I paid it back and thought he hadn't noticed. He knew all the time. From then on he had me where he wanted me. He used to sit there like a spider. I'd hand him a paper. He'd wet his thumbs with a clicking noise and a sort of complacent grimace. Click, click. Then he'd thumb the papers. He knew it drove me crazy. He'd look at me and then . . . click, click. And then he'd say something about the cash. He'd never quite accused me, just hinted. And I was impotent. You think I'm insane. I'm not. I could have murdered him. Often and often I've thought how I'd do it. Now you think I've done it. I haven't. There's the joke of it. I hadn't the pluck. And last night when Phillipa showed me she cared, it was like Heaven—unbelievable. For the first time since I've been here I *didn't* feel like killing him. And last night someone else *did!*"

He stood there trembling and vehement. Fox and Bailey, who had watched him with bewildered concern, turned to Alleyn. He was about to speak when Chase came in. "A note for you, sir," he said to Alleyn. "It came by hand."

Alleyn opened it and glanced at the first few words. He looked up.

"You may go, Mr. Hislop. Now I've got what I expected—what I fished for."

When Hislop had gone they read the letter.

Dear Alleyn,

Don't arrest Hislop. I did it. Let him go at once if you've arrested him and don't tell Phips you ever suspected him. I was in love with Isabel before she met Sep. I've tried to get her to divorce him, but she wouldn't because of the kids. Damned nonsense, but there's no time to discuss it now. I've got to be quick. He suspected us. He reduced her to a nervous wreck. I was afraid she'd go under altogether. I thought it all out. Some weeks ago I took Phips's key from the hook inside the front door. I had the tools and the flex and wire all ready. I knew where the main switchboard was and the cupboard. I meant to wait until they all went away at the New Year, but last night when Hislop rang me I made up my mind to act at once. He said the boys and servants were out and Phips locked in her room. I told him to stay in his room and to ring me up in half an hour if things hadn't quieted down. He didn't ring up. I did. No answer, so I knew Sep wasn't in his study.

I came round, let myself in, and listened. All quiet upstairs, but the lamp still on in the study, so I knew he would come down again. He'd said he wanted to get the midnight broadcast from somewhere.

I locked myself in and got to work. When Sep was away last year, Arthur did one of his modern monstrosities of paintings in the study. He talked about the knobs making good pattern. I noticed then that they were very like the ones on the radio and later on I tried one and saw that it would fit if I packed it up a bit. Well, I did the job just as you worked it out, and it only took twelve minutes. Then I went into the drawing-room and waited.

He came down from Isabel's room and evidently went straight to the radio. I hadn't thought it would make such a row, and half expected someone would come down. No one came. I went back, switched off the wireless, mended the fuse in the main switchboard, using my torch. Then I put everything right in the study.

There was no particular hurry. No one would come in while he was there and I got the radio going as soon as possible to suggest he was at it. I knew I'd be called in when they found him. My idea was to tell them he had died of a stroke. I'd been warning Isabel it might happen at any time. As soon as I saw the burned hand I knew that cat wouldn't jump. I'd have tried to get away with it if Chase hadn't gone round bleating about electrocution and burned fingers. Hislop saw the hand. I daren't do anything but report the case to the police, but I thought you'd never twig the knobs. One up to you.

I might have bluffed through if you hadn't suspected Hislop. Can't let you hang the blighter. I'm enclosing a note to Isabel, who won't forgive me, and an official one for you to use. You'll find me in my bedroom upstairs. I'm using cyanide. It's quick.

I'm sorry, Alleyn. I think you knew, didn't you? I've bungled the whole game, but if you will be a supersleuth . . . Goodbye.

Henry Meadows

☙ | Phyllis Bentley

The development of the detective as a "character" is an essential part of the detective story. Willard Huntington Wright, who wrote detective stories under the name of S. S. Van Dine and was a historian of the genre, said that the detective is the most important and original element of the criminal-problem story. "It is difficult to describe his exact literary status, for he has no counterpart in any other fictional genre. He is, at one and the same time, the outstanding personality of the story (though he is concerned in it only in an *ex-parte* capacity), the projection of the author, the embodiment of the reader, the *deus ex machina* of the plot, the propounder of the problem, the supplier of the clues, and the eventual solver of the mystery. The life of the story takes place in him, yet the life of the narrative has its being outside of him. In a lesser sense, he is the Greek Chorus of the drama. All good detective stories have had for their protagonist a character of attractiveness and interest, of high and fascinating attainments—a man at once human and unusual, colorful and gifted."

If we substitute "she" for the word "he," we have the same brilliant description of the "lady detective."

The first woman detective to appear in print appeared in a collection of short stories published anonymously in London in 1861. She was called Mrs. Paschal. She described herself as "one of those much feared, but little known persons called lady detectives," an occupation she undertook to support herself after the death of her husband. Whether or not she was much feared, we do not know; but in any case the stories were not much read. The lady was a bore.

However, fascinating lady detectives soon made striking entrances into the literary world. The grandmother of the detective story, Anna Katherine Green, produced Violet Strange; the Baroness Orczy produced "Lady Molly of Scotland Yard," and Mary Roberts Rinehart, the founder of the "Had I But Known" school of detection, created three woman sleuths, Letitia Carberry (Tish), Louise Baring, and Nurse Hilda Adams.

The exploits of these lady sleuths are no longer engrossing. Two remarkable woman detectives, however, still are the nemesis of evil and crime; they are of course, the extraordinary Miss Marple, created by Agatha Christie, and the lesser known but equally delightful Miss Phipps, created by Phyllis Bentley, a distinguished British writer, librarian, and theatrical enthusiast, who says, "I think I may say that I have two great interests—humanity, and the enrichment of human life by culture."

A Midsummer Night's Crime

"I adore Stratford!" exclaimed Miss Phipps, taking her foot off the accelerator as the spire of the church which houses Shakespeare's bones came into sight across the green Warwickshire fields. She reflected joyously on the two tickets for the Shakespeare Memorial Theatre which nestled in her purse. "*Soul of the Age! The applause! delight! the wonder of our stage! My Shakespeare, rise!*" quoted Miss Phipps rapturously.

At this moment a van drew level with her and prepared to pass. Miss Phipps frowned. It was an insult to her new little Cardinal (in two shades of rose) that she should be passed by a small tradesman's van. Flouting the voice of conscience and the Highway Code, she put her foot down firmly on the accelerator. The Cardinal leaped forward, and Miss Phipps had a swift view of the driver of the van and his companion.

The driver, who leaned forward to scowl at her, was a roughish type in a turtle-neck sweater of dirty grey, with the largest, ugliest, most peculiarly shaped ears Miss Phipps had ever seen; his companion wore a mauve silk shirt, a rather too decorative tie, and had varnished black hair.

Miss Phipps kept her foot hard down, but the van gained and presently drew level again. For a few uncomfortable seconds the van and the Cardinal rode side by side and Miss Phipps had time to observe the vehicle, which was of a rather unusual kind. It seemed to be a box made of cream-painted boards, on which some biblical texts appeared in large black capitals. *PREPARE YE THE WAY OF THE LORD*, read Miss Phipps. *THE HOUR COMETH. EXCEPT YE REPENT YE SHALL PERISH.*

"A Gospel van!" exclaimed Miss Phipps.

She had heard of these itinerant preachers, but had never met one before. It was not a form of missionary activity which commended itself to Miss Phipps, but she had too much respect for the religion of others to scoff at the van, or to hinder its work by refusing to yield the right of way. She was raising her foot from the Cardinal's accelerator when the van rendered this unnecessary by suddenly shooting ahead.

"Curious," said Miss Phipps.

The back of the van was now presented to her view. Its glossy doors read:

THOU	BLESSED
SHALL	ARE
DELIVER	THE
ME	MEEK

"Curiouser," said Miss Phipps.

Then she rebuked herself for her cynicism. One could be truly religious without handsome ears or a knowledge of grammar, and silk shirts were not a crime, particularly in this lovely summer weather.

The van flew round a bend in the road and disappeared, and Miss Phipps drove on to Stratford-upon-Avon.

"I *adore* Stratford," said a pretty, drawling, petted voice of a type which always sent shudders down Miss Phipps' spine because it so often belonged to a discontented person. "I *adore* Stratford, Michael, but I do think this is a most *disgusting* hotel."

"It was you who wanted to come here," said a muffled male voice.

"I can't help it if I don't like it, can I?"

Miss Phipps sighed. Her novelist's psychology had not misled her, she reflected, as she drew the Cardinal carefully into line. Only a very fretful spirit would find fault with the Hathaway Hotel, for it was certainly one of the best in the town.

"Look at this alleged garage space, I ask you," continued the petted voice. "How we're ever going to get *out* of it again, I don't *know*. Oh, and here's *another* car to block us in!"

She turned and scowled at Miss Phipps, who smiled back cheerfully as she got out of her car and locked the doors. Yes, just the type I'd imagined, decided Miss Phipps: fair-haired, pretty, slender, with rather exceptionally good legs, dressed in a charming blue and green summer frock cut very low, but with a face rather too liberally made up; and she was wearing entirely too much costume jewellery (necklets and bracelets) for really good taste. Also, Miss Phipps observed with her novelist's eye, whereas the two young men and the second young woman, a pleasant bright-eyed brunette, were all helping to take the luggage from their old but well-cared-for little car, the blonde girl stood aside and did not lift a finger to help them.

"Spoiled and selfish," reflected Miss Phipps sadly. Aloud she said, "Yes, these old inn yards present quite a parking problem, especially now that modern cars have grown to such a length. I think I've left you space enough, however," she continued, stepping aside to estimate this more accurately.

"Why, it's Miss Phipps!" exclaimed the shorter, plumper, and fairer of the young men, withdrawing his head from the luggage compartment and looking up.

Miss Phipps looked affable but interrogative.

"Don't you remember me? But of course you wouldn't. But

surely you remember the Laire murder trial? In Northshire, you know? Your niece's husband's partner? You pinned it on him through a member of the Laire Thespians, don't you remember? Our amateur dramatic society, you know. I was doing a production of Henry V for them—"

"Tony Harris!" exclaimed Miss Phipps.

"That's right. Ruth, Linda, Michael—this is Miss Marian Phipps. Detective, novelist, and detective-novelist. Sorry—I've introduced you the wrong way round. My sister Linda," continued Tony, indicating the blonde. "Her husband Michael Lynn. Ruth Armstrong. We're all Laire Thespians."

"We're doing *A Midsummer Night's Dream* for our summer show, so we've all come to see the Stratford production," explained Michael.

"Tony's producing, and Linda and I are doing Helena and Hermia," added Ruth.

"How do you do?" concluded the blonde coldly, tilting her pretty little nose in the air.

"She hates anyone but herself to receive any notice," thought Miss Phipps, shaking hands warmly all round. "Poor Michael."

Michael was a kind, honest-looking young man, tallish, with ordinary brown hair and ordinary brown eyes; but that was the trouble—he was too ordinary ever to satisfy the ambitious Linda, and at present his eyes showed unhappiness.

"What about a drink to celebrate our meeting?" suggested Miss Phipps.

This was well received, and they all trooped into the Hathaway by the back entrance, Michael carrying Miss Phipps' luggage and Linda's as well as his own. They then separated to their several rooms after agreeing to meet in the bar at six o'clock prompt—but not before Miss Phipps heard Linda complain, "I don't see *why* we should have such a *wretched* little room when we booked *ages* ago; you must excuse my *saying* this, Michael, but I really *don't*."

Miss Phipps of course understood the reason perfectly: the Hathaway was an expensive hotel and Michael's resources did not stretch beyond modest accommodations.

The Hathaway, like all other Stratford hotels, served dinner at a quarter past six for the benefit of theatre-goers, and although they had barely a hundred yards to walk, most guests were punctual, for they liked to get to the theatre early—the theatre exercised so great a fascination that nearly everyone wanted to share in its excitement as quickly as possible.

Miss Phipps came down promptly at the dinner hour, and Tony and Ruth followed her very shortly. Michael appeared later, but without Linda. He looked wretched, and chain-smoked three cigarettes without speaking. They drank a round at Miss Phipps' expense, and a round at Tony's; then it was time to dine.

"You'd better go in without us. I'll wait here for Linda," said Michael, looking miserably at his watch.

"Don't make it too late, old man," said Tony.

"I'm not sure whether Linda will come to the play at all," blurted Michael.

"What, after coming all this way to see it?" exclaimed Ruth.

"Is it the same trouble as before?"

"Yes. She seems as if she just can't get over it."

"I'm afraid my sister isn't showing at her best," said Tony, turning to Miss Phipps. "You see, she hoped to play Titania for the Laire Thespians and she hasn't been cast for it."

"And wasn't it a reasonable hope?" said Linda, suddenly swishing up behind them.

She certainly looked extremely pretty and fairy-like in her ethereal white dress, which billowed quite delightfully from her small waist. It was spangled in some way with silver, which her silver shoes agreeably matched. The whole effect was striking, though perhaps a litle over-elaborate for an ordinary mid-week occasion.

Miss Phipps found herself hoping that Michael's income could stand all this finery, but from the appearance of his car she had a shrewd notion that it couldn't.

"Why can't you be satisfied with Helena, Lindy?" said her brother with some irritation. "It's a longer part."

"Oh, don't be silly, Tony. I *wanted* to play *Titania*. Any casting director but Michael would have cast *me* for it."

"I can't give every leading part in the season to my own wife!" exclaimed Michael in agony.

"I don't know what Miss Phipps will think of your *callous* disregard for my *happiness*, Michael," said Linda.

"I could not love thee (Dear) so much, Lov'd I not honour more." murmured Miss Phipps.

A tide of hot but delicate colour flooded Linda's clear cheeks.

"Please don't let Michael's excessive preoccupation with his very unimportant responsibilities make us ridiculous," she said in a haughty tone.

"Nobody can make one ridiculous but oneself," said Miss Phipps briskly.

Linda gave her a glance of unmitigated hate and led the way into the dining-room.

"Have a drink first, dear," urged Michael.

"No."

"You could take it in with you."

"No!"

Miss Phipps firmly rejected the attempts of the head waiter, who was short of tables, to seat her with the Laire Thespians, and was placed in a corner alone; it might be selfish of her, but she declined to have her evening at Stratford spoiled by Linda. For the same reason she nipped out very quickly after dinner, hoping to avoid the Laire party.

"I adore Stratford!" said Miss Phipps, strolling along happily through the balmy summer air.

Beneath the pink and white chestnuts in full flower, with the river Avon flowing softly, decked by the pure white elegance of swans, a thousand people were making their way eagerly to the great theatre. There were people of all ages, religions, colours, nationalities, from all over the world. Or at least, thought Miss Phipps, shaking her head, from all over the free world. There were Indians in their lovely gauzy saris; there were French, Germans, Italians, Japanese, Malays, Americans, Canadians, Australians, Africans, Spaniards—oh, there was just everybody!

All of them looked happy and excited; all of them were talking about Shakespeare. "This is the fifth time I've seen the *Dream*"—"I'm told the rustics are particularly good"—"The *Observer* critique was rather severe"—"It's the best children's play ever written"—"You see, my dear fellow, it's such an essentially English play; a wood near Athens is all my hat, it's English countryside really"—"Is it a play to be taken seriously? Is there any philosophic significance?"—"No, no, just sit back and enjoy the sheer fun and beauty of the thing"—"I always think this place is the quintessence of the drama."

Miss Phipps, as a novelist enjoying everybody else's enjoyment as well as her own, could have wept for sheer bliss.

Alas, she had not counted on the difference in walking speed between the young and the old—the Laire party caught up with her and it was only by slipping away onto the grass that Miss Phipps avoided them. Even so she heard occasional echoes of their talk, for Linda's high voice carried through the babble of the crowd.

"An *ugly* building—outdated now, quite *old-fashioned* really . . ."

"*Far* too many swans—they're trying to get *rid* of them . . ."

"I *do* think they might do something about these *pebbles* . . ."

"Quite a *cold* breeze . . ."

To Miss Phipps' regret they all reached the great foyer, and queued to buy the huge scarlet programmes, together. Linda was now in the process of delivering a scathing attack on the choice and dating of the five plays to be performed that year.

"It's *impossible* to see *all* the plays in *one* visit unless you stay for*ever*," she said. "Why do they so *often* perform the *same* play on *consecutive* nights?"

Michael mildly suggested the problems of staging which such an arrangement might minimize.

"Well, I think it's *too* bad. And what a draught there is in this foyer!"

"You ought to have brought a coat or at least a stole, Linda," suggested the sensible Ruth, looking at the expanse of bare, though undeniably pretty, back which Linda was offering to the evening air, and glad, Miss Phipps thought, of the opportunity to terminate Linda's diatribe, which was attracting unfavourable glances from other members of the queue.

"Yes, I do hope you won't catch cold, darling," said Michael apprehensively. "I wanted you to bring your coat."

Miss Phipps guessed at once that Linda's coat was not equal in chic to her dress.

"Would you like me to slip back to the hotel and fetch it?" went on Michael.

"No."

"It wouldn't take me more than a few minutes," pleaded Michael.

"Don't *fuss* so, Michael!" said Linda crossly.

"You needn't have frozen in your best bib and tucker tonight, Linda," said Tony in a brotherly tone. "*She* won't be here until tomorrow."

"How do you know?" said Linda quickly.

She spoke with real eagerness, forgetting her languid drawl, so that Miss Phipps wondered what woman could have aroused in her such unaffected interest.

"They told me at the reception desk at the Hathaway."

"You might have told *me*," said Linda angrily, with an involuntary glance at her fluffy skirts, which in spite of their modern uncrushability would no doubt lose some of their freshness by being squashed in a theatre seat for several hours.

The five minute bell sounded.

"Well, here we go!" exclaimed Tony.

A smile of excited happiness spread over every face, even Linda's, and the crowd surged forward. The Laire party went up to the dress circle, Miss Phipps noticed, while she had treated herself to an expensive stall.

In the moments before the play began, Miss Phipps discovered on her right two Oriental gentlemen of great decorum, who did not obtrude speech upon her but bowed and smiled in a welcoming way as she pushed past them. She was vexed with herself for having made this necessary by approaching her stall from the wrong direction; she had imagined her place nearer the centre and was just a trifle disappointed to find herself only one seat from the left aisle. But with postal booking, and a theatre habitually filled every night of the season, one just had to take what the box-office sent and be grateful.

Miss Phipps then turned to her left and received the shock of her life.

Her left-hand neighbour was Mr. Mauve Shirt from the Gospel van.

"If I used a coincidence like this in a story, Ellery Queen would never swallow it," thought Miss Phipps. "But in real life such things are always happening."

She smiled affably at Mr. Mauve (as she decided to call him), and received a somewhat chilly and uncertain contortion of the features in reply.

"You must excuse my behaving as if I knew you," said Miss Phipps in her friendliest tone—after all her white hair defended her from any imputation of attempting to pick-up—"but I saw you in your Gospel van this afternoon. On the Warwick road."

Mauve Shirt said nothing. He merely tightened his lips and glowered.

"You passed me. I was driving a little Cardinal in two shades of rose," persisted Miss Phipps, somewhat abashed and feeling the need (though she knew it was absurd) to defend herself. "Remember?"

Mauve made a slight movement which might have been taken, by a friendly critic, as an inclination of his head.

"Is your mission part of some spiritual campaign?" enquired Miss Phipps. "Or is it entirely undenominational and independent?"

"It's nothing to do with me, see?" broke out Mauve Shirt in shrill Cockney tones. "It's my friend's wot I was driving with. S'nothing to do with me reelly, see."

"Oh, I see," said Miss Phipps. She felt at once relieved and amused—relieved to know that the spiritual destinies of Stratford were not to be linked with Mr. Mauve and amused by his perky speech. "An interesting experience for you, no doubt."

Mauve Shirt gave a snort so derisive that Miss Phipps was startled, and turned to give him a longer look. But at that moment the stage lights came on and there was applause for the simple majesty of the steps and columns which set the scene. Theseus and Hippolyta entered with dignity and an attendant court, Miss Phipps was enthralled—and Mauve Shirt was forgotten.

The play flew along on the iridescent wings of Shakespeare's exquisite poetry. Titania was, of course, adorable, Oberon magnificently sinister. Ordinary mortals, it seemed, were clothed in Grecian white, royalties in white with scarlet cloaks and ornaments; rustics in whatever it had pleased God to send to their obscure abodes, thought Miss Phipps, paraphrasing Gogol; fairies in a most ethereal, incredibly transparent and beautiful tulle of deepest indigo blue, so that their every movement seemed to shimmer moonlight.

As the audience rose to go out for coffee at the interval, Miss Phipps explained this sartorial scheme to the Oriental gentlemen, who were scanning their programmes with an earnest intensity which seemed to implore guidance. They all waited, standing, for the crowd in the aisle to diminish. The Orientals were a little shocked, it seemed, by the frivolous modern levity with which Helena and Hermia were being played—such tit-for-tatting females were not their idea of Shakespeare's heroines.

"That's what *I* say," broke in an American voice, which emanated from a blue-haired lady in the row behind. "It's throwing Shakespeare out the window, that's what I say, but my niece here says this is the first time those two girls ever made any sense to her, and she has a point there, you know."

"She has indeed," approved Miss Phipps. "What is your view?" she inquired, turning to Mr. Mauve Shirt.

"Well, it's not wot I was led to expeck from Shakespeare, and that's a fack," said Mauve. "That Bottom fellow is the man for my money—he's the smart one."

At this moment the crowd yielded an opening and they all surged out into the aisle. Mauve at once slipped away like an eel and vanished.

"I'm sure she's not here tonight," said the American lady to her niece.

Miss Phipps, intrigued by this second reference to an unknown woman of importance, turned round and enquired courteously, "Excuse me, but who were you expecting?"

"Why, our Miranda Lee, of course," was the reply. "Maybe she isn't as well known to you Britishers as she is to us, but—"

"Oh, but she is!" exclaimed Miss Phipps.

"—in our country we regard her as a very great actress," concluded the American lady in a rather hurt tone.

"So do we. I've seen several of her films," said Miss Phipps hastily. "She has a very real talent."

"She's planning to do a Shakespearean series on American television, so she's visiting Stratford for new production ideas," explained the blue-haired tourist, mollified.

"At the hotel it was expected that she would arrive here tomorrow."

"Is that so? Do you hear that, Monica? Miranda Lee is expected tomorrow."

"Which hotel would that be?" asked the young niece eagerly.

"The Hathaway."

"My niece would naturally like to see Miss Lee," said the American lady. "She is something of a heroine on the college campus, you know."

"I understand," said Miss Phipps. They exchanged smiles, and understood each other to have the same views on the charming susceptibility of youth.

Miss Phipps went out to the terrace overhanging the river. It was a breath-taking spectacle. Dusk was just falling, stars began to gleam, and in the darkening Avon the lights of the theatre and the distant bridge were softly reflected. A few belated swans and a solitary boat gave variety to the scene. Happy people in gay clothes crowded the terrace and balcony, talking with animation, not of private grievances nor public problems, but of the greatest poet of all time.

Mr. Mauve Shirt was leaning over the railings in the far corner. Miss Phipps smiled a little at the sight, and feeling happy and dashing, went in to the snack bar and bought herself, not coffee but a youthful glass of orangeade. She was imbibing this through a straw with considerable gusto when over the rim of her glass she caught sight of the Laire party, seated at a distant table. They all looked more cheerful than Miss Phipps had yet seen them, and Miss Phipps, feeling good will toward all men, waved a greeting and made her way to them.

"And what do you think of this way of playing the lovers?" enquired Miss Phipps. "It brightens the girls up a good deal don't you think?"

"Yes, indeed. There's a lot more scope in Helena than Linda thought," said Tony. "You must see that, Lindy."

"Small thanks to Michael," said Linda, pouting. But she was clearly pleased. "Ruth doesn't like it," she added.

"Oh, yes, I do," said Ruth quickly. "It's only that I doubt my ability to play the part that way. It's Linda's line, not mine."

"I should very much like to see the Laire production," said Miss Phipps, diplomatically.

The bell rang and the audience trooped back into the theatre. Mr. Mauve arrived in his seat late and a trifle breathless, and seemed, Miss Phipps thought, rather bored with the proceedings until the rustics' play at the end, when he applauded Bottom's playing of Pyramus very heartily. The fairies spoke the lovely epilogue and left the stage empty in moonlight; the curtains came down and went up again many times while applause thundered from all over the house; and then the national anthem brought the audience to their feet.

Miss Phipps went out with the crowd streaming away in eager talk beneath the lighted chestnut trees. The darling *Dream* was over.

"I adore Stratford!" said Miss Phipps, lolling in a deck-chair beside the gentle Avon next morning.

The sun shone brightly, the river glittered; families with young children and every imaginable breed of dog disported themselves on the grass, the customary early morning queue outside the theatre hoping for tickets for the evening performance had just dispersed, the theatre cafes were crowded. Rowing-craft flew up and down the river, ice-cream was sold from a nearby float, and the big motor-boats waited throbbing till their quota of passengers should be complete.

Miss Phipps' happiness was not quite perfect, however; she had had a theatre ticket for last night, and she had a theatre ticket for tomorrow night, but she had no ticket for tonight. It had seemed absurd, months ago when she booked, to see *A Midsummer Night's Dream* twice, on two consecutive evenings, so she had booked once for the *Dream* and once for *Coriolanus*.

But now that she was here in Stratford, she had come under the spell; and she was beginning to feel that she would give a great deal to be going to the theatre again tonight. On an impulse she climbed out of her deck-chair and approached the box-office. But there were no tickets left, not even standing-room tickets.

"Oh, well!" said Miss Phipps wistfully.

To cheer herself up she decided to take a trip on one of the motor-boats. There was one called *Titania*, and one called *George Washington* ("Why?" wondered Miss Phipps), and one called *Swan of Avon*. It was *Titania*, however, which bore her downstream to a superb view of the church. At this point the engine was stopped and the boat drifted while fares were collected. Miss Phipps' eyes wandered, and in a quiet distant field on the far bank she was suddenly sure she saw the Gospel van parked by a grassy slope.

"I am sure I saw it," mused Miss Phipps. "That's one of those odd locutions which mean the opposite of what they say. *I'm sure I saw it* means really that I'm not sure at all. Why should the van be there? How did it get there? Was it really there? I shall walk along the left bank and find out."

When she stepped off the boat, however, it occurred to her that its name, *Titania*, was a good omen; surely it meant that she would see Titania tonight. Miss Phipps really despised all such superstitious fancies, but her longing for this to be a true portent was so great that she visited the box-office again—in vain.

"Serves me right," said Miss Phipps regretfully. "I should stick to facts, not fancies."

So she trotted off across the bridge and along the path on the far bank, to check whether the presence of the Gospel van in a remote field was fact or fancy.

It was fact; but Miss Phipps had a good deal of trouble to verify it. She turned into one or two narrow lanes and climbed one or two fences before she actually set eyes on the van, for it had been parked—"Accidentally? Intentionally? Skillfully?" wondered Miss Phipps—behind a grassy knoll.

Only from one or two widely separated spots where trees and slope connived could the van be seen. Miss Phipps approached the gate leading into the field, with the intention of walking past the van towards the river bank, for she was curious to know how a Gospel van carried on its mission from so remote a position. One could not harangue a crowd at that distance.

But perhaps the van was driven back into Stratford when the urge to sermonize overtook the man with the ugly ears. The gate clicked beneath Miss Phipps' hand and the sound must have been audible in the van, for when Miss Phipps turned towards the field again after closing the gate, the man with the ugly ears stood by the back wheel. From this distance his ears were not, of course, clearly visible, but his dirty turtle-necked sweater and something in the way he stood and looked at Miss Phipps convinced her that he was the same man.

Miss Phipps paused. She took a step forward into the field. The man, motionless and silent, regarded her. Miss Phipps hesitated. The man took a step towards her. Miss Phipps turned and fled.

She was heartily ashamed of herself for doing so.

"Disgusting cowardice!" she told herself angrily. "The onset of old age! You'll be afraid of cows next! A perfectly harmless, well-meaning citizen—a bit of a crank, perhaps, but doubtless a truly religious man—and you run away from him as if he were a thug!"

"He *is* a thug," replied Miss Phipps' inner self in a subdued tone. "His whole personality is teeming with menace. As for that Gospel van, I don't believe a word of it! The way he looked at me!"

She glanced over her shoulder apprehensively, and quickened her step. Though she had now reached the river bank, a good many of the visitors had gone to lunch and this side of the Avon seemed quiet and lonely. To her relief, the ferry was working; she crossed thankfully to the theatre side. She felt quite nervous and shaken, and accepted this as an excuse to lunch in the theatre restaurant.

As there was no matinee that afternoon, the terrace restaurant was not its usual seething mass of theatre-goers waving scarlet programmes; only a few tables were occupied and Miss Phipps easily secured a place. Under the influence of the good food and charming decor (white, black, and shocking pink), Miss Phipps grew calmer; her heart quietened, her powers of observation returned.

The head waiter now ushered into the restaurant, with great respect, a party of three. There was a man whom Miss Phipps recognized as one of the important theatre officials; there was another man, tall, handsome, dark, highly silvered at the temples, elegantly dressed in grey with a white carnation in his button-hole; there was a woman who Miss Phipps knew at once must be Miranda Lee.

Oh, yes, there was no doubt of it—she was Miranda Lee. Although she was dressed in jeans and sweater, with a band of white chiffon tied carelessly round her blonde hair, her beauty blazed, and she had that look, indefinable but unmistakable, of world-wide celebrity. Her aquiline face, her wonderful pale glossy hair, her exquisite figure, her starry violet eyes, her friendly smile revealing how perfectly at ease she was in every milieu—as Miss Phipps observed all these, she felt a pang for

Linda. This was what the poor child wished to be and never would achieve; her small-town prettiness was a candle to the sun of Miranda's beauty.

"But candles are very charming and useful things to have about the house," reflected Miss Phipps. "Easier to live with—if they are content to remain candles."

All the same she could not keep her eyes from Miranda. And a certain regret crept into her gaze.

"How difficult it always is to properly assess people of another nationality," she thought sadly.

The tall handsome man, whom Miranda called Maurice, was to Miss Phipps, indubitably and at once, a fake. Quite a few of the other guests in the restaurant must have thought the same, especially the men, as Miss Phipps saw from their embarrassed looks. The Official showed by his chilly politeness when he addressed Maurice that he despised him. Even the Laire contingent, provincial though they were, reflected Miss Phipps, would not have taken long to assess Maurice as a phony. Michael and Ruth would have seen through him in an instant. Tony in an hour—even Linda would have suspected him in a day or two.

But here was this gorgeous Miranda girl, who must have met men of every kind in her seven years of fame, taken in by this shoddy piece of work simply because he sported what she probably thought was a genuine Oxford accent.

"Smooth," thought Miss Phipps, scowling at Maurice resentfully. "Clever. Insinuating. A cadger. What is the girl thinking of? Of course," she admitted, "one can hardly blame dear Maurice for making up to Miranda. What man wouldn't, if he had the chance? It's she who ought to have more *sense*. But there," repeated Miss Phipps sadly, "it's as I say. She'd see through him at once if he were her fellow-countryman."

Alas, Maurice continued to describe the vicissitudes of their drive down from London in Miranda's powerful hired car in his liquid, resonant, imitation-upper-class tones and Miranda continued to turn those marvellous eyes admiringly upon him.

"Moving accidents by flood and field," snorted Miss Phipps. "It's an old dodge, but as Shakespeare knew, it always works—it catches the Desdemonas."

She felt so vexed that she did not wait for coffee, but stalked out and went back to the Hathaway in a huff. The result of all this—of sitting hours in the fresh air, a boat trip, a walk, a fright, a big meal, and no coffee—was that when she sat down in her bedroom and picked up a detective novel, she fell asleep and did not wake till it was late afternoon.

By the time she had had a cup of tea and was strolling beneath the chestnut trees again, the car-parks were filling, the coaches arriving, the crowds already beginning to arrive for the evening performance.

In the distance she saw the Laire party, still in day clothes, and waved to them. They turned and came towards her.

"You're still here, then?" said Miss Phipps, a little surprised after Linda's angry harangue the previous day.

"Oh, yes. We're here till Sunday, I'm glad to say," said Michael.

"The boys took two days' leave," said Ruth.

"We're seeing the *Dream* again tonight—we came to *study* the production," said Tony earnestly.

"By the way, Linda," said Miss Phipps, "your Miranda Lee has arrived. I saw her at lunch in the theatre restaurant."

"What was she wearing?" asked Linda eagerly.

Miss Phipps told her. Linda's face clouded with disappointment.

"Never mind—she'll be *en grande tenue* for the theatre tonight, I'm sure," said Miss Phipps. Linda's face brightened. "Oh, how I *wish* I had a ticket for tonight!" mourned Miss Phipps. "How foolish it was of me not to get one."

"You might still get in," said Tony with sympathy. "There's always a queue for cancellations, you know—tickets sent back at the last minute. Sometimes motor coach trips will bring back as many as six! But you'd have to go now—the queue's already forming."

Miss Phipps hesitated.

"Would you like me to go and stand for you, Miss Phipps?" offered Michael. "I'll gladly do so."

"You'd miss your dinner, Michael!" Linda protested.

Michael muttered something about that being of no consequence. Miss Phipps made up her mind.

"You're a kind boy, Michael," she said, "but I'll queue for myself, thank you."

"You'll miss your dinner," said Ruth.

"I ate a big lunch."

"Why not buy a snack and take it along with you?" suggested Tony.

"Why don't *we* buy her a snack and take it to her in the queue?" suggested Michael. "Yes, that's what we'll do. You go straight to the queue now, Miss Phipps, and we'll come to you. Girls, you go along to the Hathaway and get dressed. We'll follow later."

"Don't you dare to be late, Michael," said Linda warningly.

Miss Phipps, excited and gleeful, found herself twelfth in the queue which began on the settee in the foyer and gradually spread out through the door and round the side of the building.

"Even if I don't get a seat for the performance," she decided, munching on a sausage roll, "it's worth it as a spectacle."

For, standing at one side in a fixed position, she saw and

heard more clearly than before, the polyglot audience as it poured through the great doors.

At last it was seven o'clock and the cancellations began to come in. Miss Phipps moved to tenth in the queue. Ninth. Seventh. Fifth. A young man ahead took a cancelled standing-room ticket, and Miss Phipps was then second in the line.

The Laire party arrived. Linda in her white and silver had an unhappy yearning expression on her face, and Miss Phipps did not need to be told that she had seen Miranda Lee in the Hathaway dining-room. The other three congratulated Miss Phipps on her good chance of securing a ticket. The five minute bell rang.

"We'd better be getting to our seats," said Michael.

"Oh, no! Let's wait and see her come in," said Linda.

"But why, if it makes you unhappy to see her?"

"Don't be silly, Michael! She *doesn't* make me unhappy!" said Linda, stamping her foot.

"Well, I'm going in. Come along, Ruth," said Tony impatiently.

They had just crossed the emptying foyer and were mounting the steps when Miranda Lee arrived. Maurice accompanied her, a red carnation in the lapel of his dinner jacket. Miranda was certainly worth waiting for, thought Miss Phipps, as the actress glided across the foyer to the officials waiting to receive her, with the floating gait which was one of her special graces.

As Miss Phipps had prophesied, she was *en grande tenue*. Like Linda she wore white and silver but the similarity of colour scheme only made the difference between the girls more cruel; the diamonds at Miranda's throat and wrists, the superbly tailored bodice, the white chiffon which swirled about her shoulders, the mere cobwebs of silver thread which were her shoes— all pointed to the difference between the Parisian couturier and the Laire dressmaker, the famous beauty and the pretty little girl. Linda stood wide-eyed, the corners of her mouth drooping wistfully.

"Poor Linda!" thought Miss Phipps with a pang.

Michael evidently had the same feeling, for under the guise of urging his wife towards the stairs he put his arm around her protectively.

At this moment the girl from the box-office who had been issuing the cancellations to the queue suddenly appeared before Miss Phipps, beaming, with four back-stalls tickets in her hand. Nothing could have pleased Miss Phipps better: she had a place, yet need feel no remorse in taking it since she was not the last to benefit.

She paid and rushed to her stall just a few seconds before the performance began. The last thing she saw in the auditorium before the lights faded was Mr. Mauve Shirt, down in front, sitting in the same left-aisle seat he had occupied last night.

"Curiouser, and curiouser," thought Miss Phipps.

She forgot Mr. Mauve until the end of the interval, but then remembered his late and breathless return to his seat after the interval last night. Of course drinks, coffee, cloakroom, might easily have detained him, but Miss Phipps standing at the back of the stalls and watching shrewdly, saw that he was still absent, again late in returning.

On impulse she left the auditorium, pushed through the crowd beating back in the reverse direction, and went out through the bar towards the darkening terrace. The bar, fast emptying, was almost cleared by the time Miss Phipps reached the outer door. The terrace was quite empty—except for Mr. Mauve, who in the dim far corner was leaning over the railing.

"So you're here again tonight?" called Miss Phipps cheerfully, advancing upon him.

Mauve gave a violent start and turned towards her.

"Wot if I am?" he cried. "No business of yours, lady, is it?"

Miss Phipps had never seen a cornered rat, but what she saw now was what she had always imagined. From a perky little Cockney, Mauve had turned into something dangerous. His eyes had a sudden reddish gleam, his small pale face was contorted and savage.

"Er, no," said Miss Phipps, halting suddenly. "I was just interested, that's all. Because—"

"Then keep out," said Mauve Shirt fiercely. "Out of my way, see?"

He looked round him. The terrace was empty. Miss Phipps suddenly realized that it was, indeed, quite horribly empty. She was afraid to turn her back on him. She thought of screaming, but doubted if the bar attendants would hear her in time.

She saw that Mauve was aware of her distress. He also perceived the emptiness of the terrace. His little rat eyes gleamed. He grinned. He put his hand in his pocket and advanced upon her.

"Hi-de-ho!" called a cheerful American voice from the wire gate at the other end of the terrace.

"Hi-de-ho!" shouted Miss Phipps, running madly towards it.

The niece of the blue-haired American lady—the girl who had found Hermia and Helena making sense the night before—was standing on the steps just outside the theatre precincts.

"I hope I didn't interrupt," she said politely. "We were just passing along and saw you. I wanted to thank you for telling us Miranda Lee was to stay at the Hathaway. We dined there tonight and had a wonderful view of her."

"Thank *you*," said Miss Phipps fervently. "Must go—bell has sounded—see you tomorrow perhaps!" she cried, rushing away to the safety of the crowded foyer.

"I almost wish I were *not* in Stratford," mused Miss Phipps sadly. "If I were in Southshire, I could go and tell my suspicions to Inspector Tarrant. But to a strange policeman they would sound altogether too nebulous. In fact, they *are* altogether too nebulous," concluded Miss Phipps with a sigh, picking up her book again.

She was lying in her comfortable bed at the Hathaway, trying to soothe her harrowed nerves by reading (as usual) a detective story. She had taken care to keep amongst the crowd on leaving the theatre and had thankfully joined the Laire group as they approached the hotel. Linda was at her worst, snapping and whining, but Miss Phipps would gladly have put up with someone far worse than Linda, for the sake of the protection her company afforded. Besides, poor Linda's self-confidence had been badly shaken by her glimpses of Miranda Lee, and Miss Phipps, from previous encounters with critics of her novels, knew just how painful the experience of mauled self-confidence could be.

"Oh, well!" sighed Miss Phipps again. "It's not my affair, I suppose."

In her mood of frustration she found herself dissatisfied with the development of the plot in the novel she was reading.

"These heroines, really!" exclaimed Miss Phipps.

The telephone at her bedside rang.

"Yes?" said Miss Phipps.

"Is your car a Cardinal in two shades of rose, madam?" enquired a male voice politely, giving her the registration number.

"Yes."

"Then I am afraid I must ask you to come down and move it, madam," said the voice. "A London gentleman who has to leave very early tomorrow morning is unable to get his car out."

"I left plenty of room," began Miss Phipps.

"No doubt, madam. But other cars have probably moved in since. We have so much trouble with cars parked in the yard, madam, you wouldn't believe it."

"A few well-placed white lines would eliminate your difficulties," said Miss Phipps grimly.

"Now that's an idea worth consideration," said the voice.

"Oh, very well, I'll come down. But you'd better warn the London gentleman that it may be five minutes or so before I get there. I'm in bed—I'll have to get dressed."

"I'm exceedingly sorry, madam," murmured the voice.

Miss Phipps banged down the receiver and climbed out of bed. She surveyed herself with distaste in the mirror and began reluctantly to undo the night preparations she had so recently completed. She took the net from her hair, wiped the cream from her face, threw off her nightgown, put on a dress and coat, pulled on an easy pair of shoes, and extracted the car key from her purse. She still looked pretty frightful, she decided, but sufficiently reputable to glide through the Hathaway passages without causing too much surprise.

"Luckily the weather is fairly balmy," she thought, emerging from her room.

At the foot of the stairs, in the otherwise empty hotel foyer, sat Michael Lynn, alone and smoking.

"Linda's been so hateful he dislikes the thought of going to their room," thought Miss Phipps compassionately. "Hullo, Michael!"

"Miss Phipps!" exclaimed Michael, springing to his feet. "Is there anything wrong?"

"I must look even worse than I imagined," reflected Miss Phipps sardonically. She explained the circumstances.

"Why not let me move the car for you?" suggested Michael, crushing out his cigarette. "I'm familiar with Cardinals."

"Why, how kind of you, Michael. I should be most grateful,"

said Miss Phipps, handing him the car key. "Leave the key at the reception desk, will you? I can pick it up tomorrow morning."

She returned to her room, performed all her night preparations for the second time, lay down in bed, and again took up the mystery story.

"I have no patience," she said, re-reading a paragraph, "with these heroines who are deceived by false messages. It's a gimmick for getting the heroine into the hands of the villain, which is hopelessly out of date in the modern detective story and should never be used again. No sensible woman would ever be deceived—"

"Good Lord!" cried Miss Phipps, springing out of bed. "And I've sent Michael!"

She snatched a coat, some shoes, her electric torch, and flew downstairs. The foyer was still empty, with no clerk at the reception desk, though voices could be heard coming from a room labelled *Manager's Office*.

Miss Phipps rushed through the passages to the back entrance and burst out into the long yard, a place now almost completely in shadow, filled with darker shapes. She switched on her torch and groped among the cars to her Cardinal. She knelt down.

Yes, she was right.

The false message gimmick, stale though it was, had proved successful.

A body lay on the ground, from whose head blood was slowly oozing. Owing to Michael's kindly disposition and Linda's fretfulness, however, the body belonged not to Miss Phipps, as the assailants had planned, but to Michael.

"Help! Help!" shouted Miss Phipps, rushing back into the hotel. "A man has been murdered!"

The door of the manager's office was flung open and a confused cluster of people tumbled out. There was the plump balding manager himself; there was Miranda Lee and her Maurice; there was a uniformed police sergeant, massive and rather Dobgerryish in appearance; there was a lanky gingerish young constable; there was a very neat, lean man in plain clothes whom Miss Phipps, from her long experience of her friend Robert Tarrant, recognized as a Detective-Inspector.

"Quick! Telephone for an ambulance! Michael Lynn has been attacked and wounded."

The reception clerk flew to the telephone, the sergeant to the hotel yard.

"Is he dead?" enquired the smooth tones of Maurice.

"I don't know," said Miss Phipps. She felt fairly certain that Michael lived, but thought a good fright would hasten action.

"Can this have anything to do with the other matter?" said the manager anxiously.

"What other matter? Yes, I'm certain it has," said Miss Phipps. "It was I whom they meant to knock out, not that poor boy Michael."

"Oh? Why?" said the Detective-Inspector, giving her a sharp look.

Miss Phipps was well aware that her appearance offered nothing reassuring to an Inspector's eye. She therefore became the celebrated novelist, put on her V.I.P. manner, and said firmly, "My name is Marian Phipps. I am a writer. If you will telephone the Southshire County police, Detective-Inspector Tarrant will vouch for my *bona fides.*"

"Will you all please go in there and wait," said the Inspector, indicating the manager's office.

He herded them in and closed the door firmly. Miss Phipps at once opened it.

"Poor young Mrs. Lynn must be told," she said. "And her brother, Tony Harris. Though I think her friend Miss Ruth

Armstrong will probably be more useful. They are all staying here."

"We shall attend to all that, madam," said the Inspector curtly. "Please go in there and wait."

This time he put the constable in the room with them. The man stood with his back to the door and glowered. Miss Phipps looked about her. The manager sat in the chair behind his desk, harassed and preoccupied; he was obviously wondering what on earth his directors would say to all this. Miranda Lee, looking beautiful and calm but weary, sank gracefully to a settee. Maurice seated himself beside her and lounged back against the cushions as if he had not a care in the world; yet it seemed to Miss Phipps' shrewd eye that the hands about his knee were too tightly clasped, as if to control any nervous quivering. Miss Phipps chose a seat near the door.

"May I know what was the other matter you referred to?" she asked the manager.

He hesitated, but Miranda Lee said at once, "My diamond necklace has disappeared."

"Ah!" exclaimed Miss Phipps. "Did you lose it at the theatre?"

"Yes," said the manager quickly.

"No," said Maurice.

"Opinions differ, I see," said Miss Phipps mildly. "But you, yourself, Miss Lee—when did you first miss the necklace?"

"Not till I went up to my room," replied the actress.

"Oh, I couldn't swear to that," said Maurice.

"When she was leaving the theatre, then? Could you swear to that?"

"No—how could I? It's not my habit to gaze at Miss Lee's jewelry—I prefer to look at her face."

"Very pretty," smiled Miss Phipps. Then she added mentally, "But a lie, I'll bet my Cardinal. He had a telephone call, which could have been from Mauve Shirt about me, and he was absent from Miranda's observation twice. It could have been he who telephoned me and struck down poor Michael."

At this point in her meditations the lean Inspector, followed by the massive sergeant, came in.

"Now, madam," said the Inspector sternly to Miss Phipps. "I have checked with the Southshire police about you by telephone. Just to make certain that you really are Miss Marian Phipps, would you mind telling me the name of Detective-Inspector Tarrant's second child."

"But he has no second child!" burst out Miss Phipps indignantly.

"Just a little test question, madam," said the Inspector dryly. "I think we may accept that you are, in fact, Miss Marian Phipps."

"Very kind of you, I'm sure," said Miss Phipps, ruffled.

"Will you now please give us your account of this affair. Why did you say the attack on Mr. Lynn was meant for you? Why did you say the attack was connected with Miss Lee's necklace?"

"Well," began Miss Phipps, taking breath for her story.

"Please be brief, Miss Phipps," put in the Inspector.

"I shall be thoroughly succinct," said Miss Phipps, annoyed, "because you, Inspector, have no time to lose if you wish to apprehend the thieves and recover the necklace. Briefly, then. Yesterday I was passed on the road by what is known as a Gospel van, manned by two people who looked like knaves if ever I saw knaves. The van had on its back some very familiar biblical texts, wrongly and ungrammatically quoted. And this alleged van had a far greater speed than such a van would normally have. These three observations led me to believe that it was in fact not a genuine Gospel van but a powerful car, camouflaged.

"At the theatre last night I saw one of the van men, whom I nicknamed Mr. Mauve from the colour of his shirt. Mauve, a ratty little man of a type one would not usually find in an expensive stall, was completely ignorant of Shakespeare; he mistook that delightful fool Bottom for a sharp shrewd fellow. Unfortunately I let him know that I had seen him on the van that afternoon. Mauve returned late and breathless to his stall after the interval. This morning I saw the van parked secretly in a field, some distance from the town but close to the river. When I attempted to approach it the driver became menacing. This evening I saw Mauve again in the theatre, which struck me as curious."

"Why?" barked the Inspector.

"He was completely ignorant of Shakespeare."

"Even an ignorant man might, to lessen his ignorance, attend two consecutive performances."

"Of the same play? Highly improbable," said Miss Phipps confidently. "It occurred to me that Mauve's procedure on the previous evening had been a sort of *rehearsal* for an incident which was to occur tonight. The incident, whatever it was, had been carefully planned—Mauve's two stalls must have been booked some time ago. And a superior controlling intelligence was clearly indicated.

"I followed Mauve onto the terrace. I saw him in an attitude that suggested he was dropping something over the railings. I spoke to him. He resented my presence violently. I thought he was about to attack me, but I was saved by the unexpected approach of American acquaintances.

"Clearly Mauve disliked my presence. Why? Because I, and I alone, knew that the man who dropped something over the railings was connected with the van. Therefore, it was dangerous to him that his connection with the van should become known.

"Presently Mauve's accomplice, a man with an educated voice—not Mauve or the driver—telephoned me pretending to be the hotel clerk and lured me down to the dark car park with a message asking me to move my car. Michael Lynn, in his kindness of his heart, poor lad, went out to do the errand for me and was struck down in mistake for me. Why? Again, because it was dangerous that Mauve's connection with the van should become known and so any possibility of evidence from me must be eliminated.

"Why was I dangerous? Obviously because the over-speedy, falsely-religious van was nothing but a fake. Yet if it were only a means of escape, it was a clumsy fake, for it was so very noticeable. Therefore its appearance and size were necessary to the plan.

"It then occurred to me that the van could hold a small boat. On hearing of the theft from Miss Lee it further occurred to me that Mauve had dropped Miss Lee's necklace over the railing of the empty terrace to someone in a boat below."

There was a dumfounded silence.

"But I didn't see any horrid little man like this Mauve near me in the theatre," objected Miranda Lee.

"No? I think somebody else stole the necklace and passed it to Mauve," said Miss Phipps. "The man with the smooth voice, you know. And then off the necklace went, over the railing, and down the Avon. So that if the theft were quickly discovered and a search made, it wouldn't be found anywhere in the theatre."

"It's a strange story," said the Inspector.

"It's fantastic," said Maurice with contempt.

"You'd be surprised how fantastic human beings are, sir," said the Hathaway manager, shaking his head with a knowing air. "In my profession we learn to be surprised at nothing."

"It hangs together, however," continued the Inspector, disregarding their interruptions. "And parts of it are susceptible of proof. You might get that van traced, Sergeant."

"It probably won't be a van now. The boat and the text-painted boardings will have been left in the field, and a fast car will now be on its way to London," said the manager sadly.

"Perhaps," agreed Miss Phipps. "But Mr. Mauve Shirt and his driver think they've knocked me out, you know. So there's nobody about, they think, to put two and two together. And then again," she added with a sly smile, "I gave Mauve such a start on the terrace that I rather believe he may have missed his aim, and the necklace may now be at the bottom of the Avon. What were you saying?" she enquired of Maurice, who had given an irrepressible start.

"I said nothing," replied Maurice hoarsely.

Everyone looked at Maurice—the Inspector and Sergeant in sober calculation, Miranda Lee from wide horror-stricken eyes, the manager with a sudden impish grin. But there came an interruption. A wild scream sounded from the foyer outside. So wild, so agonized was the scream that everyone in the room sprang to their feet and the Sergeant threw open the door.

Miss Phipps ducked nimbly under his arm and ran out. Two policemen were carrying Michael to the ambulance on a stretcher. His body was limp beneath the grey blanket, his eyes closed; nevertheless Miss Phipps, to her ineffable relief, saw that he lived, and that the comparatively natural colour in his cheeks indicated his injuries were not as serious as she had feared. Linda was kneeling beside the stretcher, impeding its progress and trying to raise Michael's head.

"My poor child!" said Miss Phipps, raising her from the ground. "You must let them take him quickly to the hospital."

Linda threw herself into Miss Phipps' arms.

"I can't bear it! I can't bear it!"

"You love him very much," said Miss Phipps softly, taking the opportunity to make a point on behalf of Michael's future happiness.

Linda raised a tear-stained face, which to Miss Phipps' surprise was contorted, not with grief but with terror.

"I can't do without him," she said.

Miss Phipps sighed. Even at this moment, she reflected sadly,

Linda could experience only a selfish motion—she merely dreaded the thought of life without the continuing kindness, the ever-present protection of her husband.

A hoarse breath at Miss Phipps' shoulder caused her to turn. It was Maurice who had followed her and who now tried to edge out of the door.

"I thought so," said Miss Phipps. "And where are you going, pray? To the van and your two accomplices?"

With an angry exclamation Maurice shoved her roughly aside and ran down the street.

"Inspector!" cried Miss Phipps, tottering backwards. "Catch him!"

She might have spared her breath, however, for the whole scene had already burst into violent action. Police whistles shrilled. Several constables seemed to appear from nowhere and sprinted off at the double. Late homeward-going revellers were scattered on the street outside the hotel, and threading his way through these delayed Maurice's headlong course. The lanky constable put on speed and gained on him. Miss Phipps, riding along sedately in the ambulance with Michael and Linda, witnessed the capture.

"You've nothing on me," cried Maurice angrily, his artificially smooth tones now rough and sharp. "I haven't got your blasted diamonds."

"What about this blood on your shirt-sleeve?" said the Inspector, arriving at the appropriate moment. "Assault and battery, that's yours, my man—at the least."

"I adore Stratford!" exclaimed Miss Phipps, as from a bend in the road she caught a last glimpse of the church which housed Shakespeare's bones.

Stratford had certainly done her proud on this occasion. The mystery was solved, the three villains were in custody—Maurice,

A Midsummer Night's Crime | 211

it turned out, was a jewel thief well known to the London police, Mauve Shirt and Big Ears equally well known for petty offences. The diamond necklace had been dredged up from the bottom of the Avon. Michael and Linda were reconciled, and Linda had an anecdote of a great theatrical star on which she could live for the rest of her life. Linda had something more tangible, too.

"I shall never forgive myself for being the cause of your husband's injuries, Mrs. Lynn," Miranda Lee had said to Linda. "I'm more than thankful he is convalescing so well. I'm so very deeply indebted to him."

"I don't see that *you're* indebted to him," objected Linda, nevertheless delighted. "Miss Phipps is indebted to him, but not you."

"But if he had not gone out to Miss Phipps' car, Miss Phipps would have been attacked and knocked unconscious, and then the thieves would have escaped. They would simply have raked my necklace from the bottom of the river and gotten away with it, and Maurice would still be an accepted member of my intimate circle," said Miranda with a sad little smile. "I understand that hospitalization is free in this country, or of course your husband's medical expenses would be my responsibility. As it is, you must allow me to offer you some token of my gratitude. I say you, because from what I have seen of you and Michael, I guess your husband would prefer you to benefit rather than himself. Now is there anything which would give you special pleasure?"

"Well," said Linda, colouring happily and looking at Miss Phipps for guidance. "Well! I don't know *what* to say, I'm *sure!* I don't know whether Michael would—"

"Some small personal thing, perhaps," suggested Miss Phipps. "Something which has belonged to yourself personally, Miss Lee."

Miranda smiled her beautiful, world-famous smile.

"Take this," she said, unclasping the platinum and sapphire bracelet. "Yes, Linda, I insist . . ."

So the mystery had been solved and the necklace restored and the thieves apprehended and Miranda Lee rescued from a scoundrel and Michael and Linda made happy. And all this had been accomplished with the air, curiously enough, of the greatest poet of all time.

"*Soul of the Age!*" declaimed Miss Phipps. "*The applause! delight! the wonder of our stage! My Shakespeare, rise!* And take a bow," added Miss Phipps, pressing the accelerator.

"*Sweet Swan of Avon . . .*"

Evelyn Johnson & Gretta Palmer

Our adventure into the world of the Grande Dames of Detection started with the pioneer armchair detective and ends with another true armchair detective—you. The dedicated detective story reader enjoys nothing better than beating the writer to the solution. As a matter of fact, the detective story reader takes the same delight in intellectual puzzles as does the writer of such tales. It is a category of writing that appeals strongly to even such a great mind as that of Bertrand Russell, who said, "Anyone who hopes that in time it may be possible to abolish war should give serious thought to the problem of satisfying harmlessly the instincts we inherit from long generations of savages. For my part I find a sufficient outlet in detective stories where I alternately identify myself with the murderer and huntsman detective."

Many of our Presidents have been great detective fans; Franklin D. Roosevelt, for one, evolved a remarkable plot that was later published. Presidents Woodrow Wilson, John F. Kennedy, and even Abraham Lincoln (who once won a law case by references to a detective story with which he was acquainted) were all devotees.

In this do-it-yourself piece of detection, fingerprints are all-important. Actually it was the discovery of fingerprinting that introduced the age of detection. By the beginning of the nineteenth century, it was clear that there had to be some organized way to fight crime. It took scientific discoveries and the development of certain techniques to provide the methods for the successful apprehending of a criminal. Before 1880, for example, there were not even adequate photographic files because photography was still in its infancy. It wasn't until 1883 that a young French policeman, Bertillon, introduced an involved photographic classification of criminals.

Fingerprints were even more difficult. In India in the 1860's an English civil servant named William Herschel discovered almost by accident that no two fingerprints are alike. He used his method to ink the fingers of Indian soldiers who could not write, and then asked them to place their index finger on the receipts of their paychecks.

As so often happens, the same discovery was made at the same time by a young Scot, Henry Faulds. He wrote a letter to a magazine suggesting that this would be the ideal way to identify criminals. His letter came to the attention of Sir Francis Galton, a cousin of Charles Darwin who was trying to find some method of classification for his studies in heredity. Although he was familiar with the photographic work of Bertillon, Galton settled on fingerprints as the ideal classification. His pioneer book *Fingerprints* came out in 1892, and the age of detection was on its way.

Finger Prints Can't Lie

The morning of the day we declared war on Germany, I was aroused at one o'clock by a phone call.

"This is Mrs. Booth," said a voice. "I've heard of you and you're badly needed. Will you come over?"

I went to the address she had given, and found a nice little semi-detached villa.

"Mrs. Booth?" I asked.

"Yes," said the pleasant-faced middle-aged woman who answered the door. "But the trouble is next door. I was awakened by screams about half an hour ago coming from the Marcuses'. I knew that the Doctor had gone to Germany on his lecture trip this afternoon, so I thought I had better go over. Mrs. Marcus has been quite sick; that is why the Doctor couldn't take her with him, although he is so devoted to her, and they had been planning to make this trip together for months. I got my clothes on and ran over, and found the door closed but not locked. I went in and called the maid, Mary, and no one answered, although it was not her regular night out, and Mrs. Marcus was still in bed. I ran upstairs and found Mrs. Marcus writhing on the bed in horrible agony. She was dead a minute after I got there, and never said a word. The maid came in as she died. I called Dr. Mills and he said it looked like strychnine poisoning, so I phoned you. He is over there now."

We went over to the other house. The woman was lying in

a bed in a nicely furnished room on the second floor. Dr. Mills was bending over her, but as I came in he observed that there was no use. He pointed to a bottle of capsules on the bedside table.

"I thought I had better not touch that bottle," he said. "There are finger marks on it, and I'll guarantee it contains strychnine."

The autopsy confirmed the doctor's diagnosis. A fatal amount of strychnine was found in her stomach. Dr. Marcus's closet of poisons had been broken open and the strychnine tampered with. There were good finger prints there too. I got some excellent photographic enlargements. Nothing else in the laboratory had apparently been touched. The Doctor had had very varied tastes, evidently, as I found photographic and engraving materials as well as the most elaborate chemical and medical equipment. There were finger prints all over. I got some good ones of the Doctor's, but to make certain, I developed prints from instruments no one but he had had access to. Besides, there were no other finger prints in the laboratory except the ones I took to be his and a few I afterwards found to be Mary's. I then questioned Mary, the maid. Her story was that the Doctor had told her that she could go out that evening, as Mrs. Marcus was much better, and had given her tickets to a play. The only train she could get from London to the suburb they lived in was one that got there at twelve-two. It was a short walk from the station, and when she got to the house she heard horrible screams. She had gone up and found her mistress dying, with both Mrs. Booth and Dr. Mills there. They often left the door unlocked.

I took her finger prints, and went home. I developed all my finger prints and looked at the bottle of capsules curiously. In what I ascertained to be Dr. Marcus's handwriting, it said, "One at Bed-time." Each of the ten or fifteen capsules contained enough strychnine to kill a horse.

My finger prints were ready, so I compared them. The prints on the capsule bottle and on the poison closet were identical, and both tallied with Mary's. The Doctor's were utterly different.

I went back to the house where the tragedy had taken place, but the only important thing I found was an envelope in the waste basket in Mrs. Marcus's room, containing capsules of a harmless sedative. Mary was finally acquitted, however, as no motive was ever adduced and an English jury does not like to convict a woman on circumstantial evidence.

Several other interesting facts had come out. Dr. Marcus had been a German spy of no small importance, so it is not odd that his "lecture tour" took place just when it did, as he had in all likelihood known that war would be declared.

One day after the trial, I paid a visit to Mary. I felt somehow that there had been a mistake, and I wanted to make further investigations. My efforts at the time of the trial had been greatly hampered by the fact that her lawyer was convinced that she was guilty, and had resented what he called my misplaced zeal in trying to vindicate her. He had refused to let me see her and had convinced her that I was working against her.

With a great deal of difficulty, I managed to persuade her that I was really friendly, and begged her to allow me to question her. She finally agreed. I asked her to tell me everything she had observed in the house the day of the murder. She told me that the Doctor had wakened up at seven-thirty as he always did, and she had given him breakfast downstairs and taken a tray up to Mrs. Marcus. The Doctor had shut himself up in his laboratory from nine to twelve, and Mrs. Marcus had worked at a tapestry. The Doctor's mother had come for lunch. It seems that she detested her daughter-in-law, feeling that her constant illness was mere malingering. They had had a stormy interview until the Doctor had intervened. The old lady had spent the time while he was getting ready to leave for Germany down in the living room, while Mary helped the Doctor with his packing.

"Was the mother alone downstairs?" I asked.

"Oh, yes," said Mary.

"Was the laboratory unlocked?"

"Yes, I noticed the door was open when I went down to get a duster."

"Go on," I said.

"Then the Doctor asked his mother if she wouldn't come up and make up with his wife, as he did not want to go away and leave them estranged. He seemed terribly excited and insistent about it. He was awfully fond of his mother."

"Were the capsules there then?"

"Yes, he had just given them to her and told her to be sure and take one if she couldn't sleep, as she needed plenty of sleep. Then his mother came in and kissed his wife rather unwillingly and the Doctor and I went to tie up his luggage, and pretty soon the Doctor went down to close up his laboratory. I came down to the kitchen just before he left and found him by the stove. He was putting something in the fire. There was a terrible fire going, and I told him it was too hot. So afterwards I lowered the fire in the range, and when I took out the ashes I found it must have been some rubber gloves that he had been burning, as I found the wrist and stubs of the fingers of one although all the rest had been burnt up."

I was deep in thought. If it had been the mother-in-law, that would account for the fact that the other pills had been discovered. She had only had time to toss them in the waste basket before some one came in. But Mary's finger prints? And the rubber gloves?

There was nothing I could do at the time of my interview with Mary, but early in 1919 I determined that I would unearth Marcus and get to the bottom of the mystery. I won't stop to recount all the vicissitudes that I went through to locate him. Finally I thought I had the Doctor, anyway. The mother had died in 1917.

I took the train for Munich. On the train I studied a photograph of the Doctor that Mary had given me. It was a full-length portrait that I had ascertained from several neighbors to be a perfect likeness. He was a straight, well-built man, slender, with a fine sensitive face, a long pointed nose with sculptured nostrils and a thin-lipped mouth. The brow was high and smooth and straight. He had delicate hands with long, tapering fingers, and small feet. Mary had also given me a careful description of him. He had very fine, smooth skin, she said, and she was sure he was five-feet nine, because she had seen his passport. I would be certain to know him.

When I reached my destination, a nurse opened the door, and told me that Dr. Schwartz was out. Dr. Schwartz was the man I was sure was Marcus. She asked me to come into the waiting room and I gladly accepted the opportunity to have a look around. I was in luck, for the door to his office was open. I looked about the desk carefully, but everything there was thoroughly impersonal, except for a book which was lying open. It had markers in it and had been much thumbed. I looked at the title. *"Cushing,"* it said, *"The Pituitary Body."*

I rushed back to the waiting room, hearing footsteps, and a man came in.

He looked at me inquiringly.

"Dr. Schwartz?" I said.

"Yes," he replied.

It was not my man at all. This man was six feet tall with great rugged, craggy features. His eyes were sunk, and his brow furrowed; he had a thick heavy nose, and great pendulous lips. His skin was thick and wrinkled and pachydermatous. He had large nobby hands and huge feet. He was terribly stooped and dull-eyed.

But I wanted to be sure; so when I saw that as he talked to me about my purely imaginary ailment, he fingered his paper cutter,

I took the liberty to put it in my pocket when his back was turned.

I took out the paper cutter when I got home, and developed the beautiful finger prints with which it was covered.

They were exactly like the prints Dr. Marcus had left all over his laboratory!

Who murdered Mrs. Marcus, and how do you account for the confusion in finger prints?

THE SOLUTION

Dr. Marcus murdered his wife to prevent her from giving away his state secrets. He broke into his own poison-cabinet before his departure for Europe and placed the strychnine in a bottle from which he wiped his own finger prints. He had photographed the finger prints of Mary, had engraved them and transferred them in the positive onto a pair of rubber gloves. Wearing these gloves, he handled the bottle, leaving traces that corresponded to Mary's own hand. His instructions to his wife about the medicine insured that she would not take the poison until after he was well on his way to Europe. During the four years that elapsed before the detective reached him, he entirely changed his appearance by inducing to a marked degree a disease call acromegaly which can be brought on by eating enormous quantities of pituitary extract. Such changes as a gain of several inches in height and unrecognizably heavier features are a result of this disease.

Biographical Notes

Baroness Orczy, novelist and playwright, was born in Hungary in 1865, the only child of Baron Felix Orczy, a noted composer and conductor. Although she did not speak English until she was fifteen, all her writings are in that language. After studying in Brussels and Paris, she enrolled at the Heatherly School of Art in London, where she met a fellow student, Montagu W. Barstow, whom she married. She had a modest success as a painter and illustrator when she began writing in the late 1890s. In 1905 she won international recognition with a play, *The Scarlet Pimpernel* (written in collaboration with Barstow). A novel of the same name was published the next year and the two introduced a long series of popular "Pimpernel" successes. "The Old Man in the Corner," who made his appearance in a book of that title in 1909, gained the Baroness attention from historians of detective fiction because he is one of the earliest examples of the "armchair" school of sleuthing. She continued writing until her death in 1947 at the age of eighty-two.

Carolyn Wells, American writer, was born in Rahway, New Jersey, in 1869. She was a writer of humorous sketches, parodies, juveniles, short stories, novels, and detective fiction. Miss Wells described herself as a "jack-in-the-box brain" entirely surrounded by books. When her *The Nonsense Anthology—*

still her best-known work—was published in 1902, she had already published eight books. By the time of her death the total had increased to more than 170. Of these, more than seventy-five were mystery and detective stories, many about her famous detective Fleming Stone. Her autobiography, *The Rest of My Life*, bravely discussed her lifelong deafness brought about by an attack of scarlet fever at the age of six. Miss Wells was married to Hadwin Houghton in 1918. She died in New York City on March 26, 1942, after years of invalidism which failed to prevent her from writing.

Agatha Christie was born in 1891 in Torquay, England, of an English mother and an American father. Her first attempt at writing, toward the end of World War I, was rejected by several publishers. It was entitled *The Mysterious Affair at Styles*, and in this work she introduced the now famous Belgian detective Hercule Poirot. The book was eventually accepted and was published in 1920. In 1926, after averaging a book a year, she wrote what is still considered her masterpiece, *The Murder of Roger Ackroyd*. In private life she is Lady Mallowan, the wife of the noted British archaeologist Sir Max E. L. Mallowan, and has often accompanied him on his expeditions, using the experiences as background for some of her books. In 1971, on her eightieth birthday, her eightieth book was published. She was created a Dame Commander of the British Empire in 1971.

Dorothy Leigh Sayers, writer of detective stories, was born in 1893 at Oxford, where her father was a headmaster. Educated at Somerville College, she was one of the first women to get an Oxford degree. She married Oswald Atherton Fleming in 1926. Her first detective story, *Whose Body?*, was published in 1923, and introduced her now famous young nobleman detective,

Lord Peter Wimsey, modeled on one of the more popular dons of her day. In addition to her original work, she is known throughout the world for her three anthologies, *Omnibuses of Crime* (in England, *Great Short Stories of Detection, Mystery, and Horror*). She also wrote a number of plays. Miss Sayers died in 1957.

Margery Allingham, British writer, was born in London, England, in 1904, the daughter of Herbert John, a writer. She started writing at the age of seven and produced her first published novel at sixteen. From then on until her death in 1966, she produced suspense and detective novels which earned her an international reputation. Her husband, Philip Youngman Carter, always discussed her work with her and completed her last book after her death.

Celia Laighton Thaxter, American poet, was born in Portsmouth, New Hampshire, in 1835. Her father, Thomas B. Laighton, became keeper of the White Island lighthouse in the Isles of Shoals, a small island group off the coast of Portsmouth. Successive homes on these small barren shoals provided the background for her poems *Driftweed* (1879) and other volumes and for the prose *Among the Isles of Shoals* (1873). She married Levi Lincoln Thaxter in 1851 and spent most of her life on Appledore, one of the Isles of Shoals. She died in 1894.

Ngaio Marsh was born in Christchurch, New Zealand, in 1899. She was educated at Canterbury University College School of Art. She has spent much of her life in the theater, as an actress, manager, and drama lecturer. Miss Marsh wrote her first detective novel in 1932 while in London. That same year she returned to New Zealand and has lived there and in

London, writing detective novels and taking an active part in repertory theater work.

Phyllis Bentley, English novelist, was born in Halifax, England, in 1894, the daughter of Joseph Edwin, a cloth manufacturer of great skill and reputation. She was educated at the Halifax High School and at the Cheltenham Ladies College, and received her B.A. degree in London in 1914. She is a librarian, a drama critic, and regional novelist as well as a writer of detective fiction.

Evelyn Johnson and *Gretta Palmer* were early collaborators on the book *Murder*. However, it was their only collaboration and Miss Johnson's only book. Gretta Palmer continued to write short stories, articles, and books on the feminist movement. She was a foreign correspondent in Indochina in the 1940s, and died in 1953.